"Frank, shocking . . . extremely sympathetic, penetrating and exhortive. . . . Few readers will put this book down unmoved or untaught." —*New York Herald Tribune*

"*The City and the Pillar* had the courage to subject American masculinity, in all its parochialism, to the kind of scrutiny that only one who dared to be himself, like Gore Vidal, could achieve. This is a novel about original sin, American style." —Bernard F. Dick, author of *The Apostate Angel: A Critical Study of Gore Vidal*

"A serious work of literature. The theme is most sensitively handled, the writing, always sober and responsible, quickens often to a lyrical tone, and the detail is closely observed. . . . Impressive." —*The Spectator*

"Remarkable. . . . A compelling story written in elegantly spare prose. . . . Wonderfully mythic." —Jay Parini in *Gore Vidal: Writer Against the Grain*

"A remarkable and characteristically courageous achievement. At once a penetrating study of self-deception and an unsentimental analysis of gay life in the 1940s, it traces convincingly a young man's awakening while also locating this experience in the vast expanses and repetitive patterns of myth." —Claude J. Summers, author of *Gay Fiction: Wilde to Stonewall—Studies in a Male Homosexual Literary Tradition*

"A brilliant exposé of subterranean life." —*The Atlantic Monthly*

GORE VIDAL

THE CITY AND THE PILLAR

Gore Vidal was born in 1925 at the United States Military Academy at West Point. His first novel, *Williwaw,* written when he was nineteen years old and serving in the Army, appeared in the spring of 1946. He subsequently wrote twenty-three novels, five plays, many screenplays, short stories, well over two hundred essays, and two memoirs. He died in 2012.

INTERNATIONAL

BOOKS BY GORE VIDAL

NOVELS
Williwaw
In a Yellow Wood
The City and the Pillar
The Season of Comfort
A Search for the King
Dark Green, Bright Red
The Judgment of Paris
Messiah
Julian
Washington, D.C.
Myra Breckinridge
Two Sisters
Burr
Myron
1876
Kalki
Creation
Duluth
Lincoln
Empire
Hollywood
Live from Golgotha
The Smithsonian Institution
The Golden Age

NONFICTION
Inventing a Nation

SHORT STORIES
A Thirsty Evil
Clouds and Eclipses

PLAYS
An Evening with Richard Nixon
Weekend
Romulus
On the March to the Sea
The Best Man
Visit to a Small Planet

ESSAYS
Rocking the Boat
Reflections Upon a Sinking Ship
Homage to Daniel Shays
Matters of Fact and of Fiction
The Second American Revolution
At Home
Screening History
United States
The Last Empire
Perpetual War for Perpetual Peace
Imperial America
The Selected Essays of Gore Vidal

MEMOIRS
Palimpsest
Point to Point Navigation

THE CITY AND THE PILLAR

THE CITY
AND THE PILLAR

A Novel

▼

GORE VIDAL

VINTAGE INTERNATIONAL

Vintage Books • *A Division of Random House, Inc.* • *New York*

FIRST VINTAGE INTERNATIONAL EDITION, DECEMBER 2003

Copyright © 1948, 1965 by E. P. Dutton & Co., Inc.
Introduction copyright © 1995 by Literary Creation Enterprises, Inc.

The Cataloging-in-Publication data is on file at the Library of Congress.

Vintage ISBN: 1-4000-3037-4

www.vintagebooks.com

Printed in the United States of America
12 14 16 18 20 19 17 15 13

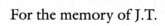

For the memory of J.T.

But his wife looked back from behind him
and she became a pillar of salt.

INTRODUCTION

Much has been made—not least by the Saint himself—of how Augustine stole and ate some pears from a Milanese orchard. Presumably, he never again trafficked in, much less ate, stolen goods, and once this youthful crime ("a rum business," snarled the unsympathetic American jurist Oliver Wendell Holmes, Jr.) was behind him, he was sainthood bound. The fact is that all of us have stolen pears; the mystery is why so few of us rate halos. I suspect that in certain notorious lives there is sometimes an abrupt moment of choice. Shall I marry or burn? Steal or give to others? Shut the door on a life longed for while opening another, deliberately, onto trouble and pain because . . . The "because" is the true story seldom told.

My father once told me, after reviewing his unpleasant period in public office, that whenever it came time for him to make a crucial decision, he invariably made the wrong one. I told him that he must turn to Churchill and write his own life, demonstrating what famous victories he had set in motion at Gallipoli or in the "dragon's underbelly" of the Third Reich. But my father was neither a writer nor a politician; he was also brought up to tell the truth. I, on the other hand, was brought up by a politician grandfather in

Washington, D.C., and I wanted very much to be a politician, too. Unfortunately, nature had designed me to be a writer. I had no choice in the matter. Pears were to be my diet, stolen or homegrown. There was never a time when I did not make sentences in order to make those things that I had experienced cohere and become "real."

Finally, the novelist must always tell the truth as he understands it while the politician must never give the game away. Those who have done both comprise a very short list indeed. The fact that I was never even a candidate for the list had to do with a choice made at twenty that entirely changed my life.

At nineteen, just out of the army, I wrote a novel, *Williwaw* (1946): it was admired as, chronologically, at least, the first of the war novels. The next year I wrote the less admired *In a Yellow Wood* (1947). Simultaneously, my grandfather was arranging a political career for me in New Mexico (the governor was a protégé of the old man). Yes, believe it or not, in the greatest democracy the world has ever known—freedom's as well as bravery's home—elections can be quietly arranged, as Joe Kennedy liked to explain to you.

For someone twenty years old I was well situated in the world, thanks to two published novels and my grandfather's political skills. I was also situated dead center at a crossroads rather like the one Oedipus found himself at. I was at work on *The City and the Pillar*. If I published it, I'd take a right turn and end up accursed in Thebes. Abandon it and I'd turn left and end up in holy Delphi. Honor required that I take the road to Thebes. I have read that I was too stupid at the time to know what I was doing, but in such matters I have always had a certain alertness. I knew that my description of the love affair between two "normal" all-American boys of the sort that I had spent three years with in the wartime army would challenge every superstition about sex in my native land—which has always been more Boeotia, I fear, than Athens or haunted Thebes. Until then, American novels of "inversion" dealt with transvestites or with lonely bookish boys who married unhappily and pined for Marines. I broke that mold. My two lovers in this novel were athletes and so drawn to the entirely masculine that, in the case of one, Jim Willard, the feminine was simply irrelevant to his passion to unite with his other half, Bob Ford: unfortunately for Jim, Bob had other sexual plans, involving women and marriage.

I gave the manuscript to my New York publishers, E. P. Dutton. They hated it. One ancient editor said, "You will never be forgiven for this book. Twenty years from now you will still be attacked for it." I responded with an uneasy whistle in the dark: "If any book of mine is remembered in the year 1968, that's real fame, isn't it?"

To my grandfather's sorrow, on January 10, 1948, *The City and the Pillar* was published. Shock was the most pleasant emotion aroused in the press. How could our young war novelist . . . ? In a week or two, the book was a bestseller in the United States and wherever else it could be published—not exactly a full atlas in those days. The English publisher, John Lehmann, was very nervous. In his memoirs, *The Whispering Gallery*, he writes, "There were several passages in *The City and the Pillar*, a sad, almost tragic book and a remarkable achievement in a difficult territory for so young a man, that seemed to my travellers and the printers to go too far in frankness. I had a friendly battle with Gore to tone down and cut these passages. Irony of the time and taste: they wouldn't cause an eyebrow to be lifted in the climate of the early sixties." But only twenty years ago the book was taken from Dennis Altman as he arrived at the airport in Sydney, Australia. Altman challenged the obscenity law under which the book had been seized. The judge in the case acknowledged that under the law that he must administer the book was obscene, but then, in a famous obiter dicta, he wrote that he thought the law absurd: in due course, it was changed. Meanwhile, even today, copies of the book still fitfully blaze on the pampas and playas of Argentina and other godly countries.

What did my confreres think? I'm afraid not much. The fag writers were terrified; the others were delighted that a competitor had so neatly erased himself. I did send copies to two famous writers, fishing, as all young writers do, for endorsements. The first was to Thomas Mann. The second was to Christopher Isherwood, who responded enthusiastically. We became lifelong friends. Through Joseph Breitbach I was told that André Gide was planning to write an "appreciation," but when we finally met he spoke only of a handwritten, fetchingly illustrated pornography that he had received from an English clergyman in Hampshire.

At fourteen I had read Thomas Mann's *Joseph* books and realized that the "novel of ideas" (we still have no proper phrase for this sort of book or, indeed, such a genre) could work if one were to set a narrative within history. Later, I was struck by the use of dialogue in *The Magic Mountain*, particularly the debates between Settembrini and Naphta, as each man subtly vies for the favors of the dim but sexually attractive Hans Castorp. Later, there would be complaints that Jim Willard in *The City and the Pillar* was also dim. But I deliberately made Jim Willard a Hans Castorp type: what else could someone so young be, set loose in the world—the City—that was itself the center of interest? But I did give Jim something Hans lacked: a romantic passion for Bob Ford that finally excluded everything else from his

INTRODUCTION ▲ XV

life, even, in a sense, the life itself. I got a polite, perfunctory note from Thomas Mann, thanking me for my "noble work": my name was misspelled.

Contemplating the American scene in the 1940s, Stephen Spender deplored the machinery of literary success, remarking sternly that "one has only to follow the whizzing comets of Mr. Truman Capote and Mr. Gore Vidal to see how quickly and effectively this transforming, diluting, disintegrating machinery can work." He then characterized *The City and the Pillar* as a work of sexual confession, quite plainly autobiography at its most artless. Transformed, diluted, disintegrated as I was, I found this description flattering. Mr. Spender had paid me a considerable compliment; although I am the least autobiographical of novelists, I had drawn the character of the athlete Jim Willard so convincingly that to this day aging pederasts are firmly convinced that I was once a male prostitute, with an excellent backhand at tennis. The truth, alas, is quite another matter. The book was a considerable act of imagination. Jim Willard and I shared the same geography, but little else. Also, in the interest of verisimilitude I decided to tell the story in a flat gray prose reminiscent of one of James T. Farrell's social documents. There was nothing fancy in the writing. I wanted the prose plain and hard.

In April 1993, at the State University of New York at Albany, a dozen papers were read by academics on *The City and the Pillar*. The book has been in print for half a century, something I would not have thought possible in 1948, when *The New York Times* would not advertise it and no major American newspaper or magazine would review it or any other book of mine for the next six years. *Life* magazine thought that the greatest nation in the country, as Spiro Agnew used to say, had been driven queer by the young army first mate they had featured only the previous year, standing before his ship. I've not read any of the Albany papers. For one thing, it is never a good idea to read about oneself, particularly about a twenty-one-year-old self who had modeled himself, perhaps too closely, on Billy the Kid. I might be shot in the last frame, but I was going to take care of a whole lot of folks who needed taking care of before I was done.

There were those who found the original ending "melodramatic." (Jim strangles Bob after an unsuccessful sexual encounter.) When I reminded one critic that it is the nature of a romantic tragedy to end in death, I was told that so sordid a story about fags could never be considered tragic, unlike, let us say, a poignant tale of doomed love between a pair of mentally challenged teenage "heteros" in old Verona. I intended Jim Willard to demonstrate the romantic fallacy. From too much looking back, he was destroyed, an unsophisticated Humbert Humbert trying to re-create an idyll that never truly existed except in his own imagination. Despite the title, this was never plain in the narrative. And of course the coda *was* unsatisfactory. At the time it was generally believed that the publishers forced me to tack on a cautionary ending in much the same way the Motion Picture Code used to insist that wickedness be punished. This was not true. I had always meant the end of the book to be black, but not as black as it turned out. So for a new edition of the book published in 1965 I altered the last chapter considerably. In fact, I rewrote the entire book (my desire to imitate the style of Farrell was perhaps too successful), though I did not change the point of view or the essential relationships. I left Jim as he was. He had developed a life of his own outside my rough pages. Claude J. Summers noted that of the characters only Jim Willard is affecting, and he commands sustained interest largely because he combines unexpected characteristics. Bland and ordinary, he nevertheless has an unusually well-developed inner life. Himself paralyzed by romantic illusions, he is surprisingly perceptive about the illusions of others. For all the novel's treatment of him as a case history, he nevertheless preserves an essential mystery. As Robert Kiernan comments (*Gore Vidal*), Jim Willard is Everyman and yet he is l'étranger . . .* the net effect is paradoxical but appropriate for it decrees that, in the last analysis, we cannot patronize Jim Willard, sympathize with him entirely, or even claim to understand him. Much more so than the typical character in fiction, Jim Willard simply exists, not as the subject of a statement, not as the illustration of a thesis, but simply as himself.

Not long ago I received a telephone call from the biographer of Thomas Mann. Did I know, he asked, the profound effect that my book had had on Mann? I made some joke to the effect that at least toward the end of his life he may have learned how to spell my name. "But he didn't read the book until 1950, and as he read it he commented on it in his diaries. They've just been published in Germany. Get them." Now I have read, with some amazement, of the effect that Mann's twenty-one-year-old admirer had on what was then a seventy-five-year-old world master, situated by war in California.

Wednesday 22, XI, 50
. . . Began to read the homo-erotic novel "The City and

---

*Claude J. Summers in "The Cabin and the River" (*Gay Fictions*, New York: Continuum, 1990) quotes from Robert F. Kiernan's book *Gore Vidal* (New York: Frederick Ungar, 1982).

the Pillar" by Vidal. The day at the cabin by the river and the love-play scene between Jim and Bob was quite brilliant.—Stopped reading late. Very warm night.

Thursday 23, XI, 50

. . . Continued "City and Pillar."

Friday 24, XI, 50

. . . In the evening continued reading "The City and the Pillar." Interesting, yes. An important human document, of excellent and enlightening truthfulness. The sexual, the affairs with the various men, is still incomprehensible to us. How can one sleep with men—[Mann uses the word *Herren*, which means not "men" but "gentlemen." Is this Mann being satiric? A rhetorical question affecting shock?].

Saturday evening 25, XI, 50

. . . in May 1943, I took out the *Felix Krull* papers only to touch them fleetingly and then turn to *Faustus*. An effort to start again must be made, if only to keep me occupied, to have a task in hand. I have nothing else, no ideas for stories; no subject for a novel. . . . Will it be possible to start [*Felix Krull*] again? Is there enough of the world and are there enough people, is there enough knowledge available? The homosexual novel interests me not least because of the experience of the world and of travel that it offers. Has my isolation picked up enough experience of human beings, enough for a social-satirical novel?

Sunday 26, XI, 50

Busy with [the *Krull*] papers, confusing.

Read more of Vidal's novel.

Wednesday 29, XI, 50

. . . The *Krull* papers (on imprisonment). Always doubts. Ask myself whether this music determined by a "yearning theme" is appropriate to my years. . . . Finished Vidal's novel, moved, although a lot is faulty and unpleasant. For example, that Jim takes Bob into a Fairy Bar in New York.

I am pleased that Mann did not find the ending "melo-dramatic," but then what theme is more melodramatically "yearning" than *Liebestod*? In any case, the young novelist who took what seemed to everyone the wrong road at Triv-ium is now saluted in his own old age by the writer whom he had, in a certain sense, modeled himself on. As for Mann's surprise at how men could sleep with one another, he is writing a private diary, the most public act any German master can ever do, and though he often refers to his own "inversion" and his passions for this or that youth, he seems not to go on, like me, to Thebes but to take (with many a backward look) the high road to Delphi. I am duly aston-ished and pleased that, as he read me, he was inspired—motivated—whatever verb—to return to his most youthful and enchanting work, *Felix Krull*, which features some-thing of a lighter, more allegro version of my own Jim Willard in the guise of a character whom he appropriately called Felix—the Latin for "happy."

THE CITY AND THE PILLAR

CHAPTER

1

THE MOMENT WAS STRANGE. There was no reality in the bar; there was no longer solidity; all things merged, one into the other. Time had stopped.

He sat alone in a booth, listening to the music which came out of a red plastic box, lighted within. Some of the music he remembered from having heard it in other places. But the words he could no longer understand. He could recall only vague associations as he got drunk, listening to music.

His glass of whiskey and water and ice had slopped over and the top of the table was interesting now: islands and rivers and occasional lakes made the top of the table a continent. With one finger he traced designs on the wooden table. He made a circle out of a lake; he formed two rivers from the circle; he flooded and destroyed an island, creating a sea. There were so many things that could be done with whiskey and water on a table.

The jukebox stopped playing.

He waited a long time for it to start again. He took a swallow of the whiskey to help him wait. Then after a long time, in which he tried not to think, the music started. A record of a song he remembered was playing and he allowed himself to be taken back to that emotional moment in time when . . . when? He tried hard to remember the place and the time, but it was too late. Only a pleasant emotion could be recalled.

He was drunk.

Time collapsed. Years passed before he could bring the drink to his mouth. Legs numb, elbows detached, he seemed to be supported by air, and by the music from the jukebox. He wondered for a moment where he was. He looked about him but there were no clues, only a bar in a city. What city?

He made a new island on the tabletop. The table was his home and he felt a strong affection for the brown scarred wood, for the dark protectiveness of the booth, for the lamp which did not work because there was no bulb in the socket. He wanted never to leave. This was home. But then he finished his drink, and was lost. He would have to get another one. How? He frowned and thought. A long time went by and he did not move, the empty glass in front of him.

At last he came to a decision. He would leave the booth and go talk to the man behind the bar. It was a long voyage but he was ready for it.

He stood up, became dizzy, and sat down again, very tired. A man with a white apron came over to his table; he probably knew about liquor.

"You want something?"

Yes, that was what he wanted, something. He nodded and said slowly so that the words would be clear, "Want some whiskey, water, bourbon, water . . . what I been drinking."

The man looked at him suspiciously. "How long you been here?"

He didn't know the answer to that. He would have to be sly. "I have been here for one hour," he said carefully.

"Well, don't go passing out or getting sick. People got no consideration for others when it comes to doing things like that for other people to clean up."

He tried to say that he did have consideration for others but it was no use. He could not talk anymore. He wanted to get back home, to the tabletop. "I'm OK," he said, and the man went away.

But the top of the table was no longer home. The intimacy had been dispelled by the man with the apron. Rivers, lakes, islands, all were unfamiliar; he was lost in a new country. There was nothing for him to do except turn his attention to the other people in the barroom. Now that he had lost his private world, he wanted to see what, if anything, the others had found.

The bar was just opposite him and behind it two men in white aprons moved slowly. Four five six people stood at the bar. He tried to count them but he could not. Whenever he tried to count or to read in a dream, everything dissolved. This was like a dream. Was it a dream?

A woman wearing a green dress stood near him, large buttocks, dress too tight. She stood very close to a man in a dark suit. She was a whore. Well well well. . . .

He wondered about the other booths. He was at the center of a long line of booths, yet he knew nothing about the people in any of them. A sad thought, to which he drank.

Then he stood up. Unsteadily, but with a face perfectly composed, he walked toward the back of the barroom.

The men's room was dirty and he took a deep breath before he entered so that he would not have to breathe inside. He saw himself reflected in a cracked distorted mirror hung high on the wall. Blond hair, milk white, bloodshot eyes staring brightly, crazily. Oh, he was someone else all right. But who? He held his breath until he was again in the barroom.

He noticed how little light there was. A few shaded bulbs against the walls and that was all, except for the jukebox, which gave not only light but wonderful colors. Red blood, yellow sun, green grass, blue sky. He stood by the jukebox, his hands caressing the smooth plastic surface. *This* was where he belonged, close to light and color.

Then he was dizzy. His head ached and he could not see clearly; stomach contracted with sharp nausea.

He held his head between his hands and slowly he pushed out the dizziness. But then he pushed too hard and brought back memory; he had not wanted to do that. Quickly he returned to the booth, sat down, put his hands on the table, and looked straight ahead. Memory began to work. There had been a yesterday and a day before, and twenty-five years of being alive before he found the bar.

"Here's your drink." The man looked at him. "You feeling all right? If you don't feel good you better get out of here. We don't want nobody getting sick in here."

"I'm all right."

"You sure had a lot to drink tonight." The man went away.

He had had a lot to drink. It was past one and he had been in the bar since nine o'clock. Drunk, he wanted to be drunker, without memory, or fear.

"You all by yourself?" Woman's voice. He didn't open his eyes for a long time, hoping that if he could not see her she could not see him. A basic thing to wish but it failed. He opened his eyes.

"Sure," he said. "Sure." It was the woman in the green dress.

Her hair was dyed a dark red and her face was white with powder. She too was drunk. She leaned unsteadily over his table and he could see between her breasts.

"May I sit down?"

He grunted; she sat opposite him.

"It's been an awfully hot summer, hasn't it?" She made conversation. He looked at her, wondering if he could ever assimilate her into the world of the booth. He doubted it. For one thing, there was too much of her, and none of it simple.

"Sure," he said.

"I must say you're not very talkative, are you?"

"Guess not." The intimacy of the booth was gone for good now. He asked, not caring, "What's your name?"

She smiled, his attention obtained. "Estelle. Nice name, isn't it? My mother named all of us with names like that. I had one sister called Anthea and my brother was called Drake. I think Drake is a very attractive name for a man, don't you? He's in women's wear. What's your name?"

"Willard," he said, surprised that he was giving her his right name. "Jim Willard."

"That's a nice name. Sounds so English. I think English names are attractive. In origin I'm Spanish myself. Oh, I'm thirsty! I'll call the waiter for you."

The waiter, who seemed to know her, brought her a drink. "Just what the doctor ordered." She smiled at him. Under the table her foot touched his. He moved both feet under his chair.

She was not distressed. She drank rapidly. "You from New York?"

He shook his head and cooled his forefinger in the half-empty glass.

"You sound sort of Southern from the way you talk. Are you from the South?"

"Sure," he said, and he took his forefinger out of the glass. "I'm from the South."

"It must be nice down there. I've always wanted to go to Miami but I never seem to get away from the city. You see, all my friends are here and I can't very well leave them. I did have a friend once, a man," she smiled privately, "and he always went to Florida in the winter. He had beautiful luggage. He invited me to go down with him and I almost went, once." She paused. "That was ten years ago." She sounded sad, and he didn't pity her at all.

"Of course it must be terribly hot there in the summer. In fact, it's so hot *here* that I think sometimes I'll *die* from the heat. Were you in the war?"

He yawned, bored. "I was a soldier."

"I'll bet you look good in a uniform. But I'm glad it's finally over, the war."

He moved his glass around the table, listening to the satisfying noise it made as it hit scars and cracks. She watched him. He wished she would go away.

"Why're you in New York?" she asked. "And why are you getting drunk? You got everything and still you're sitting here all by yourself, getting drunk. I wish *I* was you. I wish I was young and nice-looking. I wish . . ." Quietly she began to cry.

"I got everything," he said, sighing. "I got everything, Anthea."

She blew her note in a piece of Kleenex. "That's my sister's name, Anthea. I'm Estelle."

"And you have a brother named Drake."

She looked surprised. "That's right. How did you know?"

Suddenly he felt himself in danger of becoming involved in her life, hearing confessions, listening to names that meant nothing to him. He shut his eyes, tried to shut her out.

She stopped crying and took a small mirror out of her handbag. Tenderly she powdered the pouches under her eyes. Then she put the mirror away and smiled. "What're *you* doing tonight?"

"I'm doing it. Drinking."

"No, silly, I mean later. You're staying in a hotel somewhere, maybe?"

"I'm staying right here."

"But you can't. It closes at four."

Alarm. He had not thought what he was going to do after four o'clock. It was her fault. He had been happily listening to music, until she came along and changed everything. It had been a mistake, not assimilating her.

She menaced him with reality. She must be destroyed.

"I'm going home alone," he said. "When I go home, I go home alone."

"Oh." She thought a moment, decided on injury and hurt. "I suppose I'm not good enough for you."

"Nobody is." He was mortally weary of her, and sick at the thought of sex.

"Pardon me," said Estelle, sister of Anthea and Drake. She stood up, arranged her breasts, and returned to the bar.

Now he was alone and he was glad, with three glasses before him on the table: two empty, one half full with lipstick on it. He arranged the glasses to form a triangle, but then when he tried to arrange them to form a square, he failed. Why? Three glasses ought to be able to form a square. He was distressed. Fortunately, reality began to recede once more. And Jim Willard sat at his table in his booth in his barroom and made lakes, rivers, islands. This was all that he wanted. To be alone, a creature without memory, sitting in a booth. Gradually, the outline of fear grew blurred. And he forgot entirely how it began:

CHAPTER
2

I

ON THE WARMEST AND greenest afternoon of the spring, the high school's commencement exercises ended, and boys and girls, parents and teachers, streamed out of the brand-new Old Georgian school building. Separating himself from the crowd, Jim Willard paused a moment on the top step and looked out, searching for Bob Ford. But he could not make him out in the mob of boys in dark jackets and white trousers, girls in white dresses, fathers in straw hats (this year's fashion in Virginia). Many of the men smoked cigars, which meant that they were politicians—this was the county seat and singularly rich in officeholders, among them Jim's father, the courthouse clerk.

A running boy struck Jim's arm playfully. Jim turned, expecting Bob. But it was someone else. He smiled, struck back, and exchanged cheerful insults, secure in the knowledge that he was popular because he was the school's tennis champion and all athletes were admired, particularly those who were modest and shy, like Jim.

At last Bob Ford appeared. "This year me. Next year you."

"I sure wish it was me who just graduated."

"I feel like they opened the prison door and let me out into the great big world. So how did I look up there on that stage wearing that black potato sack?"

"Great."

"Don't you know it?" Bob chuckled. "Well, come on. We better play while we still got some light." As they moved through the crowd to the door to the locker room, a dozen girls greeted Bob, who responded with an easy grace. Tall, blue-eyed, with dark red curling hair, he was known throughout the school as Lover Man, a phrase somewhat more innocent than it sounded. "Love" meant little more than kissing. Most girls found Bob irresistible, but boys did not much like him, possibly because girls did. Only Jim was his friend.

As they entered the dim locker room, Bob looked about him with a delighted melancholy. "I guess this is the last time I'll be coming in here."

"Well, we can still use the courts this summer. . . ."

"That's not what I meant." Bob took off his coat and hung it up carefully. Then he took off his tie. These were his best clothes and he handled them with respect.

"What do you mean?" Jim was puzzled. But Bob merely looked mysterious.

The two boys walked the half mile to the tennis courts without speaking. They had known each other all their lives but it was not until this last year that they had become close friends. They had been on the baseball team together and they had played tennis together, even though Jim always won, to Bob's chagrin. But then Jim was the best player in the county, and one of the best in the state. Games had been particularly important to both of them, especially for Jim, who found it difficult to talk to Bob. The hitting of a white ball back and forth across a net was at least a form of communication and better than silence or even one of Bob's monologues.

They had the red-clay courts to themselves. Bob spun a racket and Jim, the loser, took the side facing the sun. The game began. It was good to hit the white ball evenly, making it skim the net. Jim played his best, obscurely aware that this was a necessary ritual enacted for the last time.

They played while the sun set and the shadows of tall trees lengthened, darkening the court. A cool breeze stirred. After the third set, they stopped. Jim had won two out of three.

"Nice going," said Bob, and gave him his hand briefly, as though they were in a tournament. Then they both stretched out on the grass beside the court and breathed deeply, tired but comfortable.

Twilight and the day ended. Chattering birds circled among the trees, preparing for night.

"It's getting late." Bob sat up, brushing away the twigs and leaves that had stuck to his back.

"It's still light." Jim did not want to go.

"I hate to leave, too." Bob looked about, again the mysterious sadness.

"What're you talking about? You been hinting around all day. What're you up to?" Then Jim understood. "You're not going to ship out on a boat, are you? Like you said last year?"

Bob grinned. "Curiosity killed the cat."

"OK." Jim was hurt.

Bob was contrite. "Look, I can't say anything just now. Whatever it is, I'll tell you before Monday. That's a promise."

Jim shrugged. "It's your business."

"I got to get dressed." Bob stood up. "I'm taking old Sally Mergendahl to the dance tonight." He winked. "And tonight I mean to do myself some good."

"Why not? Everybody else has." Jim disliked Sally, a dark aggressive girl who had been after Bob all year. But then it was none of his business what Bob did.

As they walked through the blue twilight to the school, Bob suddenly asked, "What're you doing this weekend?"

"Nothing. Why?"

"Why don't we spend it down at the cabin?"

"Well, sure. Why not?" Jim was careful not to show too much pleasure; it was bad luck. The cabin had been the home of a onetime slave, recently dead. It stood deserted now, in thick woods close to the Potomac. Once they had spent a night there; more than once Bob had brought girls to the cabin. Jim was never certain exactly what happened because Bob's stories varied with each telling.

"OK," said Bob. "Meet you at your house, tomorrow morning."

An irritable janitor let them into the locker room.

II

BREAKFAST WAS INVARIABLY UNPLEASANT, possibly because it was the only meal the Willard family always had together.

Mr. Willard was already at the head of the table when Jim came into the dining room. Small, thin, gray, Mr. Willard tried to appear tall and commanding. It was the family's opinion that he would have had no trouble at all being elected governor, but for one reason or another he had been forced to allow lesser men to go to Richmond while he remained at the courthouse, a bitter fate.

Mrs. Willard was also small and gray but inclined to fat; after twenty-three years of her husband's stern regime, she had assumed the melting look of the conscious martyr. Now wearing a white frilled apron which did not become her, she cooked breakfast in the adjoining kitchen, looking from time to time into the dining room to see if her three children were down.

Jim, the firstborn son, was first to appear. Since this was a special day, he was cheerful, glad to be alive.

"Morning, Father."

His father looked at him as though he could not quite place the face. Then he said, "Good morning," and distantly started to read the paper. He discouraged conversation between himself and his sons, especially Jim, who had made the error of being tall and handsome and not at all the sort of small, potentially gray son Mr. Willard ought to have had.

"You're down early." Mrs. Willard brought him his breakfast.

"Beautiful day, that's why."

"I don't think a quarter to eight is such an early hour," said his father from behind the *Richmond Times.* Mr. Willard had been brought up on a farm and one of the reasons for his life's success had been rising "at the crack of dawn."

"Jim, you didn't hear any funny noises around the house last night, did you?" Like Joan of Arc, his mother was always hearing funny noises.

"No, ma'am."

"Funny, I could've sworn someone was trying to get in the window; there was this tapping. . . ."

"I should like some more coffee, if I may." Mr. Willard lowered his newspaper and raised his chin.

"Of course, dear."

Jim ate his cereal. Mr. Willard rearranged his newspaper.

"Good morning." Carrie came into the room. A year older than Jim, she was pretty but pale, and disliking paleness, painted her face with a bold and imaginative hand, which sometimes made her look whorish and infuriated her father. She had graduated from high school the year before, at seventeen, a fact which the family impressed on Jim. Since then, she helped her mother in the house while encouraging the attentive courtship of a young realtor whom she expected to marry just as soon as he had "put something by."

"Morning, Carrie." Mr. Willard looked at his daughter with wintry approbation. Of his children, she alone gave him pleasure; she saw him great.

"Carrie, will you come in here and help me with breakfast?"

"Yes, Mother. How was the graduation, Jim?"

"OK."

"I wish I could have gone but I don't know why it is, I'm so busy all the time, on the go. . . ."

"Sure, sure."

Carrie joined her mother in the kitchen and Jim could hear them arguing in low voices; they always argued. Finally, John entered. At fourteen, he was thin, nervous, potentially gray, except for black eyes.

"Hi." He sat down with a crash.

"Glad to have you with us," said his father, continuing the war.

"It's Saturday." John was a skilled domestic warrior, master of artillery. "Everybody sleeps late."

"Naturally." Mr. Willard looked at John and then, satisfied in some strange way with what he saw, returned to his paper.

Carrie brought her father more coffee and then sat down beside Jim. "When do you start work in the store, Jimmy?"

"Monday morning." He wished she wouldn't call him Jimmy.

"That'll be nice. It's sort of dull, I guess, but then I suppose you have to be *qualified* to do more skilled work, like in an office, typing."

He didn't answer her. Neither Carrie nor his father could irritate him today. He was meeting Bob. The world was perfect.

"Hey, they're playing baseball today over at the school. You going to play?" John struck his fist against his palm with a satisfactory sound.

"No, I'm going down to the cabin. For the whole weekend."

Mr. Willard struck again. "And who, if I'm not asking too much, are you going with?"

"Bob Ford. Mother said it was all right."

"Is that so? It is amazing to me why you want to sleep away from your own home which we have tried at such expense to make comfortable. . . ." His father slowly unfurled the domestic banner, and charged. Jim refused to defend himself, beyond promising himself that one day he would throw a plate at this bitter old man he was forced to live with. Meanwhile, he simply stared at his future weapon while his father explained to him how the family was a Unit and how he owed all of them a Debt and how difficult a time Mr. Willard had had making the Money to support them and though they were not rich, they were Respectable, and Jim's going around with the son of the town drunk did them no good.

During her husband's tirade Mrs. Willard joined them, a demurely pained expression on her face. When Mr. Willard had finished, she said, "Well, I think the Ford boy is nice and he does get good marks in school and his mother *was* a friend of ours no matter what we think of the father. So I don't see anything wrong with Jim seeing him."

"*I* don't mind," said Mr. Willard. "I just thought *you* would mind having your son exposed to that sort of a person. But if you don't, I have nothing more to say." Mr. Willard, having embarrassed his son and disagreed with his wife, ate fried eggs with unusual gusto.

Mrs. Willard murmured something soothing and Jim wished that his father were like Bob's father, drunk and indifferent.

"When are you going to the cabin?" his mother asked, in a low voice, so as not to disturb her husband.

"After breakfast."

"And what are you doing about food?"

"Bob's getting stuff from the store where he works."

"That's nice," said Mrs. Willard, obviously thinking of something else; she had a difficult time concentrating for very long.

Carrie and her younger brother started arguing and soon breakfast was finished. Then Mr. Willard rose and announced that he had business at the courthouse, which was not true. The courthouse never did business on Saturday. But his wife did not question this and, with a reserved nod to his children, Mr. Willard put on his straw hat, opened the front door, and stepped out into the bright morning.

Mrs. Willard watched him a moment, expressionless; then she turned and said, "Carrie, come help me clean up. Boys, you better fix your room."

The boys' room was small and not very light. The two

beds, close together between two bureaus, made the room crowded. Pictures of baseball and tennis players covered the walls, early idols of Jim's.

John had no idols. He was intense and studious and he was going to be a Congressman, which pleased his father, who often gave him talks on how to be a success in politics. Jim had no plans beyond college. It all seemed a long way off.

Jim made his bed quickly; John took longer.

"What're you and Bob going to do down by the river?"

"I don't know." Jim straightened the patchwork quilt. "Fish. Loaf."

"That sounds like a waste of time." John echoed his father.

"Isn't that too bad?" Jim mocked as he opened the closet and took down two blankets from the shelf, his contribution to the weekend.

John sat on the bed and watched. "Bob sees a lot of Sally Mergendahl, doesn't he?"

"I suppose so. She sees a lot of people."

"That's what I mean." John looked knowing and Jim laughed.

"You're too young to be hearing such things."

"Like hell I am." John proved his virility with an oath.

"Sure, you're a real lover and you keep track of all the girls."

John was angry. "Well, that's more than you do and you're older than me. You don't ever go out with girls. I heard Sally say once she thought you were the best-looking guy in school and she couldn't understand why you didn't go around more. She said she thought you were afraid of girls."

Jim flushed. "She's full of crap. I'm not afraid of her or

anybody. Besides, I do my traveling on the other side of town."

"Really?" John was interested and Jim was glad he had lied.

"Sure." He was mysterious. "Bob and me go over there a lot of times. All the baseball team does, too. We don't want to mess around with 'nice' girls."

"I guess not."

"Besides, Sally isn't so fast."

"How do you know?"

"I just do."

"I'll bet Bob Ford said that about her."

Jim fixed the top of his bureau, ignoring his brother. He was ill at ease and he didn't know why; it was seldom that John could irritate him.

Jim looked in the dusty mirror above his bureau and wondered if he needed his weekly shave. He decided that he could wait till he got back. Absently he ran his hand over his short blond hair, glad that it was summer, the season of short hair. Was he handsome? His features were perfectly ordinary, he thought; only his body pleased him, the result of much exercise.

"When's Bob coming by?" John was sitting on his bed, balancing his brother's tennis racket in his hand.

"Right now."

"Must be nice down there. I was only to the cabin once. I guess anybody can go there."

"Sure."

"They say the guy who owns the land lives in New York and he never comes down here. I'm playing baseball this afternoon and then I'm going to a meeting of the Democratic Party in the back of the drugstore." John's mind was quick and unsettled.

"That must be a lot of fun." Jim put his racket in the closet. Then he picked up the two blankets and went downstairs.

Carrie was in the sitting room, lazily dusting furniture.

"Oh, *there* you are, Jim."

He stopped. "Anybody looking for me?"

"No, I just said there you were." She put the duster down, glad of an excuse not to work. "Are you going to the high-school dance tonight?"

He shook his head.

"That's right," she said, "you and Bob are going to the cabin. I'll bet Sally is jealous of you for keeping him from coming to the dance."

Jim didn't let his face change expression. "It was his idea," he said evenly. "Maybe you'll find out *why* later." Mystery was clearly the order of the day.

Carrie nodded. "I think I know. I've been hearing stories about Bob's going away. Sally said something about it not so long ago."

"Maybe he is, maybe he isn't." Jim was surprised that Carrie and Sally knew; he wondered how many other people Bob had told.

Carrie yawned and began to dust again. Blankets under his arm, Jim went to the kitchen. His mother was not yet finished cleaning.

"Now be sure you're back by Sunday night. Your grandfather's coming over and your father will want you to be here. Are those the good blankets you're taking?"

"No, old."

Through the kitchen window Jim saw Bob carrying a large paper bag.

"I'm on my way."

"Look out for water moccasins!"

The morning sun was hot, yet the air was cool. The day was green and blue and very bright. Jim Willard was meeting Bob and the weekend was not yet lived. He was happy.

III

THEY STOOD ON THE edge of the cliff and looked down at the brown river, muddy from spring rains and loud where it broke up on the black rocks in midstream. Below them, the cliff dropped steeply to the river, a wall of stone, dark green with laurel and wild grapevines.

"Must be a flood upstream. That old river looks mean," said Bob.

"Maybe we'll see a house come floating down."

Bob chuckled. "Or a privy." Jim sat on a rock and plucked a piece of long grass and chewed on the white sweet-tasting stem. Bob squatted beside him. Together they listened to the roar of the river and the noise of tree frogs and the rustle of bright new leaves in the wind.

"How was Sally?"

Bob growled. "Prick-teaser, like all the rest. Leads you on so you think, *now* I can lay her and then, just as you get all hot, *she* gets scared: Oh, what're you doing to me? Oh, stop! You stop that now!" Bob sighed with disgust. "I tell you it makes a man so horny he could lay a mule, if it would just stand still." Bob contemplated mules. Then: "Why didn't you come to the dance last night? Lots of girls asked for you."

"I don't know. Don't like dancing, I guess. I don't know."

"You're too bashful."

Bob rolled up a trouser leg and removed a large black

ant, which was crawling up his calf. Jim noticed how white Bob's skin was, like marble, even in the sun.

Then, to break the silence, they threw stones over the edge of the cliff. The sound of rock hitting rock was entirely satisfying. Finally Bob shouted, "Come on!" And they crawled over the edge of the cliff and cautiously worked their way downward, holding on to bushes, finding toe-holds in the rock.

The hot sun shone in a pale sky. Hawks circled while small birds flashed between trees. Snakes, lizards, rabbits all scuttled for cover as the boys made their noisy descent. At last they reached the river's muddy bank. Tall black rocks jutted from brown sand. Happily, they leapt from rock to rock, never once touching earth, stepping only on the relics of a glacier age.

Shortly after noon they came to the slave cabin, a small house with a shingled roof much perforated by weather. The interior smelled of rotted plaster and age. Yellow news-papers and rusty tin cans were scattered over the rough wood floor. On the stone hearth there were new ashes: tramps as well as lovers stayed here.

Bob set down the paper bag he had been carrying while Jim put the blankets on the cleanest part of the floor.

"Hasn't changed much." Bob looked up at the roof. The sky shone through holes. "Let's hope it don't rain."

Close to the cabin there was a large pond, bordered by willows and choked with lilies. Jim sat on the moss-covered bank while Bob undressed, throwing his clothes into a nearby tree, the trousers draped like a flag on one branch while his socks hung like pennants from another. Then he stretched happily, flexing his long muscles and admiring himself in the green smooth water. Though slim, he was strongly built and Jim admired him without envy. When

Bob talked of someone who had a good build, he invariably sounded envious; yet when Jim looked at Bob's body, he felt as if he were looking at an ideal brother, a twin, and he was content. That something was lacking did not occur to him. It seemed enough that they played tennis together and Bob spoke to him endlessly of the girls he liked.

Cautiously Bob put one long foot in the water. "It's warm," he said. "Real warm. Come on in." Then, hands on knees, he leaned over and studied his own reflection. As Jim undressed, he tried to fix the image of Bob permanently in his mind, as if this might be the last time they would ever see one another. Point by point, he memorized him: wide shoulders, narrow buttocks, slim legs, curved sex.

Naked, Jim joined Bob at the water's edge. The warm breeze on his bare skin made him feel suddenly free and curiously powerful, like a dreamer who is aware that he is dreaming.

Bob looked at him thoughtfully. "You got a good tan. I sure look white. Hey!" He pointed at the water. Below the dark green surface, Jim could see the blunt slow-moving shape of a catfish. Then, suddenly, he was falling and there was a rush of water in his ears. Bob had pushed him in. Choking, he came to the surface. With a rapid movement, Jim grabbed Bob's leg and pulled him in. Grappling, they turned and twisted in the water, making the pond foam. As they wrestled, Jim took pleasure in the physical contact. So, apparently, did Bob. Not until both were exhausted did they stop.

For the rest of that day they swam, caught frogs, sunned themselves, wrestled. They talked little. Not until the light began to fail did they relax.

"It's sure nice here." Bob stretched out full length. "I guess there isn't any place as nice and peaceful as this place is." He patted his flat stomach and yawned.

Jim agreed, totally at peace; he noticed that Bob's belly quivered with the regularity of a pulse. He looked at himself: the same phenomenon. Before he could comment on it, he saw a tick heading toward his pubic hair. He pinched it hard until it popped.

"I got a tick."

Bob jumped to his feet. Ticks gave you a fever, so they examined themselves carefully, but found nothing. They got dressed.

The air was gold. Even the gray walls of the cabin looked gold in the last light of the sun. Now they were hungry. Jim built a fire while Bob made hamburgers in an old frying pan. He did everything easily, expertly. At home he cooked for his father.

They ate their supper, sitting on a log facing the river. The sun had gone. Fireflies darted like yellow sparks in the green shadow of the woods.

"I'm going to miss this," said Bob finally.

Jim looked at him. In the stillness there was no sound but the rushing river. "My sister said Sally said you were going to leave right after graduation. I told her I didn't know anything about it. Are you going?"

Bob nodded and wiped his hands on his trousers. "Monday, on the Old Dominion Bus Line."

"Where are you going to go?"

"To sea."

"Like we always talked about."

"Like we always talked about. Oh, I tell you I'm fed up with this town. The old man and I don't get along at all and God knows there isn't anything to do around here. So I'm going. You know I never been out of this county, except to go over to Washington. I want to see things."

Jim nodded. "So do I. But I thought we were going to

go to college first and *then* we would . . . well, you would go off on this trip."

Bob caught a firefly in his hand and let it climb up his thumb, and fly away.

"College is too much work," he said at last. "I'd have to work my way through and that means a job, which means I'd never get a chance to play around. Besides, there isn't a thing they could teach me that I want to know. All I want is to travel and to hell around."

"Me too." Jim wished that he could say what he wanted to say. "But my father wants me to go to college and I suppose I got to. Only I'd hoped we could go together . . . well, team up in tennis doubles. We could be state champions. Everybody says so."

Bob shook his head and stretched out. "I got to get moving," he said. "I don't know why but I do."

"I feel the same way, sometimes." Jim sat beside Bob on the ground and together they watched the river and the darkening sky.

"I wonder what New York is like," said Bob at last.

"Big, I guess."

"Like Washington. That sure is a big town." Bob rolled over on his side, facing Jim. "Hey, why don't you come with me? We can ship out as cabin boys, maybe even deckhands."

Jim was grateful Bob had said this, but he was cautious by nature. "I think I ought to wait till next year when I get that high-school diploma, which is important to have. Of course my old man wants me to go to college. He says I should . . ."

"Why do you pay any attention to that bastard?"

Jim was shocked and delighted. "Well, I don't really. In fact, I'd just as soon never see him again." With surprising ease, he obliterated his father. "But even so, I'm scared, going off like that."

"Nothing to it." Bob flexed the muscles of his right arm. "Why, a guy like you with brains and a good build, he can do most anything he wants. I knew these guys, they were sailors out of Norfolk, and they said there was nothing to it; easy work and when you're onshore you have a good time all the time, which is what I want. Oh, I'm tired of hanging around this town, working in stores, going out with *nice* girls. Only they're not really so damned nice, they're just afraid of getting knocked up." Fiercely he struck the ground with his fist. "Like Sally! Why, she'd do anything to you you want except the one thing you got to have. And that sure makes me mad. She makes me mad. All the girls around here make me mad!" Again he struck the dark earth.

"I know how it is," said Jim, who did not know how it was. "But aren't you scared you'll catch something from somebody you meet in New York?"

Bob laughed. "Man, I'm careful!" He turned over on his back.

Jim watched the fireflies rise from the nearby grass. It was already night. "You know," he said, "I wish I could go with you up North. I'd like to see New York and do as I please for once."

"So why don't you?"

"Like I said, I'm afraid to leave home and the family, not that I like them all that much but . . ." His voice trailed off uncertainly.

"Well, you can come with me if you want to."

"Next year, after I graduate, I'll come."

"*If* you can find me. I don't know where I'll be by then. I'm a rolling stone."

"Don't worry. I'll find you. Anyway, we'll write."

Then they walked down to the narrow boulder-strewn beach. Bob scrambled onto a flat rock and Jim followed him. The river swirled about them as they sat side by side in the blue, deep night.

One by one, great stars appeared. Jim was perfectly contented, loneliness no longer turning in the pit of his stomach, sharp as a knife. He always thought of unhappiness as the "tar sickness." When tar roads melted in the summer, he used to chew the tar and get sick. In some obscure way he had always associated "tar sickness" with being alone. No longer.

Bob took off his shoes and socks and let the river cool his feet. Jim did the same.

"I'll miss all this," said Bob for the dozenth time, absently putting his arm around Jim's shoulders.

They were very still. Jim found the weight of Bob's arm on his shoulders almost unbearable: wonderful but unbearable. Yet he did not dare move for fear the other would take his arm away. Suddenly Bob got to his feet. "Let's make a fire."

In a burst of activity, they built a fire in front of the cabin. Then Bob brought the blankets outside and spread them on the ground.

"There," he said, looking into the yellow flames, "that's done." For a long moment both stared into the hypnotically quivering flames, each possessed by his own private daydream. Bob's dream ended first. He turned to Jim. "Come on," he said menacingly. "I'll wrestle you."

They met, grappled, fell to the ground. Pushing and pulling, they fought for position; they were evenly matched, because Jim, though stronger, would not allow Bob to lose or to win. When at last they stopped, both were panting and sweating. They lay exhausted on the blanket.

Then Bob took off his shirt and Jim did the same. That was better. Jim mopped the sweat from his face while Bob stretched out on the blanket, using his shirt for a pillow. Firelight gleamed on pale skin. Jim stretched out beside him. "Too hot," he said. "Too hot to be wrestling."

Bob laughed and suddenly grabbed him. They clung to one another. Jim was overwhelmingly conscious of Bob's body. For a moment they pretended to wrestle. Then both stopped. Yet each continued to cling to the other as though waiting for a signal to break or to begin again. For a long time neither moved. Smooth chests touching, sweat mingling, breathing fast in unison.

Abruptly, Bob pulled away. For a bold moment their eyes met. Then, deliberately, gravely, Bob shut his eyes and Jim touched him, as he had so many times in dreams, without words, without thought, without fear. When the eyes are shut, the true world begins.

As faces touched, Bob gave a shuddering sigh and gripped Jim tightly in his arms. Now they were complete, each became the other, as their bodies collided with a primal violence, like to like, metal to magnet, half to half and the whole restored.

So they met. Eyes tight shut against an irrelevant world. A wind warm and sudden shook all the trees, scattered the fire's ashes, threw shadows to the ground.

But then the wind stopped. The fire went to coals. The trees were silent. No comets marked the dark lovely sky, and the moment was gone. In the fast beat of a double heart, it died.

The eyes opened again. Two bodies faced one another where only an instant before a universe had lived; the star burst and dwindled, spiraling them both down to the meager, to the separate, to the night and the trees and the firelight; all so much less than what had been.

They separated, breathing hard. Jim could feel the fire on his feet and beneath the blanket he was now uncomfortably aware of small stones and sticks. He looked at Bob, not certain of what he would see.

Bob was staring into the fire, face expressionless. But he grinned quickly when he saw Jim watching him. "This is a hell of a mess," he said, and the moment fled.

Jim looked down at himself and said as casually as he could, "It sure is."

Bob stood up, the firelight glittering on his body. "Let's wash up."

Pale as ghosts in the dark night, they walked to the pond. Through the trees they could see the light from their fire, yellow and flickering, while frogs croaked, insects buzzed, river thundered. They dove into the still black water. Not until they had returned to the fire did Bob break the silence. He was abrupt.

"You know, that was awful kid stuff we did."

"I suppose so." Jim paused. "But I liked it." He had great courage now that he had made his secret dream reality. "Did you?"

Bob frowned into the yellow fire. "Well, it was different than with a girl. And I don't think it's right."

"Why not?"

"Well, guys aren't supposed to do that with each other. It's not natural."

"I guess not." Jim looked at Bob's fire-colored body, long-lined and muscular. With his newfound courage, he put his arm around Bob's waist. Again excited, they embraced and fell back onto the blanket.

Jim woke before dawn. The sky was gray and the stars were fading. The fire was almost out. He touched Bob's arm and watched him wake up. They looked at one another. Then Bob grinned and Jim said, "You're still going Monday?"

Bob nodded.

"You'll write me, won't you? I'd like to get on the same boat with you next year."

"Sure, I'll write you."

"I wish you weren't going . . . you know, after this."

Bob laughed and grabbed him by the neck. "Hell, we got all day Sunday." And Jim was satisfied and happy to have all day Sunday with this conscious dream.

CHAPTER
3

I

BOB WROTE ONE LETTER from New York: things had been
tough but now it looked as if he'd be shipping out on the
American Export Line. Meanwhile, he was having a swell
time and had met a lot of girls, ha-ha. Jim replied promptly,
only to have his letter returned, "Addressee unknown."
There was no second letter. Jim was hurt but not entirely
surprised. Bob was not much of a letter writer, particularly
now that he was absorbed in that new life which they would
soon share, for Jim had already made up his mind that once
high school was done with, he would follow Bob to sea.

On the greenest and the warmest day of the next June,
Jim graduated from high school and began a two week's
battle with his father. Jim won. He would go to New York
for the summer and work, with the understanding that in
the fall he would return to Virginia and enter college. Natu-

rally, he would have to work his way through the university, but it was not every father who was willing to offer his son that opportunity. And so, early one bright yellow morning, Jim kissed his mother, shook his father's hand, said a casual good-bye to his brother and sister, and got on the bus to New York with seventy-five dollars in his pocket, more than enough, he reckoned, to keep him until he found Bob.

New York was hot, gray, dirty. Jim found it astonishing (where did all those people come from? Where were they all hurrying to?) and oppressive in the summer heat. But then he was not a tourist. He was on a quest. After renting a room at a YMCA he went to the Seamen's Bureau, where he learned that there was no record of a Bob Ford. For a moment he experienced panic. But then one of the old-timers explained to him that men often shipped out using other men's papers. In any case, the best thing for him to do was to apply for a berth as a cabin boy. Sooner or later, he and Bob would meet. The sea was surprisingly small; paths always crossed. Jim was put on a list. There would be a wait, perhaps a long one. While his papers cleared, he visited bars, got drunk twice (and disliked it), saw dozens of movies, and became an interested spectator of the life of the street. Then, just as his money ran out, he was signed on a freighter as cabin boy.

The sea was a startling experience. It took time to get used to the constant throb of engines beneath steel bulkheads, the slap and fall of a ship going full speed into the wind, the close confinement in the fo'c'sle with thirty strangers, foulmouthed but for the most part amiable. He ended by enjoying the life. In Panama he learned that a deckhand named Bob Ford had recently passed through the port, on his way to San Francisco. Jim's luck was improving.

He transferred to a cargo ship bound for Seattle by way of San Francisco. But the trail ended in San Francisco. He could find no trace of Bob. Disconsolately, he roamed the city and visited waterfront bars, hoping for a sudden glimpse of Bob. Once he thought he saw him at the far end of a bar, but when he approached, heart beating fast, the figure turned toward him and showed a stranger's face.

Jim signed on as cabin boy aboard the Alaska Line and spent the rest of the year at sea. Entirely absorbed in his new life, he no longer wrote to his parents. Only the absence of Bob shadowed the full days he spent aboard ship during that first snow-bright winter of his freedom.

On Christmas Day the ship was off the coast of south-eastern Alaska, headed for Seattle. Jagged mountains rose from black water. The sea was heavy, the wind rising. Those passengers who were not sick were having breakfast in the dining saloon. They sat at round tables and made brave jokes about the motion of the ship and their fallen comrades, while the messboys hurried back and forth between galley and saloon, carrying heavy china plates of food.

Only one of Jim's passengers had come to breakfast. She was a plump, thick woman with bad skin. She was very jovial. "Good morning, Jim," she said brightly. "Nasty weather, isn't it? I suppose all the landlubbers are sick."

"Yes, ma'am." He began to clear away the remains of her breakfast.

"Me, I've never felt better." She inhaled the close cabin air. "This weather agrees with me." She patted herself and glanced at Jim as he picked up his tray. "When are you going to fix that porthole thing of mine, the thing that's broken and keeps rattling all the time?"

"I'll try, when I make up your cabin."

"That'll be fine," said the plump woman and she left the

table, swaying slightly as she walked, using what she called her "sea legs."

Jim took the tray back to the galley. Breakfast was over. The steward dismissed him. Whistling to himself, Jim walked down the companionway to a small cabin aft where he found Collins, a short, square young man of twenty with dark curly hair, blue eyes, and a love of himself which was surprisingly contagious. On his left arm he had an intricate vein-blue tattoo which pledged him forever to Anna, a girl belonging to the dim past, when he was sixteen and living in Oregon, not yet a seaman. Collins was sitting on an upright box, smoking.

"Hello, boy," said Collins.

Jim grunted and sat down on another box. He took a cigarette out of Collins's shirt pocket and then lit it with his own match.

"Only two more days," said Collins, "and then . . ." He rolled his eyes and made obscene designs in the air. "Can't wait to get back to Seattle. Hey, what've they got planned for today? You know it's Christmas."

"Sure, I got a calendar, too," said Jim callously.

"I wonder," said Collins more specifically, "if we'll get any liquor. This is the first time I ever been to sea at Christmas. Some ships, foreign ships mostly, serve liquor to the men."

Jim exhaled sadly. "I don't think they will," he said, watching the smoke fade. "But we ought to get some truck from the passengers."

"Hope so." Collins yawned. "By the way, how you doin' with the hog?" The messboys enjoyed kidding Jim about the plump woman at his table. Her interest in him was hardly secret.

Jim laughed. "I keep her in deep suspense."

"Wonder if she's got any money. You might pick up some

extra change there." Collins was serious, and Jim was disgusted, but he didn't show it because Collins was his best friend aboard ship. Also, Jim was never sure if Collins really did the things he said he did or not.

"I'm not that hungry," said Jim.

Collins shrugged. "I always need money. All the time I need it and now we're going to Seattle I'll need a lot more than I got. Well, maybe somebody rich'll die and leave it to me." Collins was essentially a thief, but it was good policy to appear to have illusions about shipmates. Besides, Collins was guide as well as friend. He had made Jim's life easier aboard ship by showing him different ways to avoid work, as well as places like this cabin to hide in.

Jim stretched. "I got to start making beds."

"Plenty of time. Steward won't be looking for you for a while." Collins stamped out his cigarette butt and quickly lit another. Jim finished his own cigarette. He disliked smoking. But aboard ship it was important to keep your hands busy when there was nothing to do, and in his months at sea there were days on end when there was little to do, except listen to the men talk of women and ships' officers, of good ports and bad. And once each man had said what he had to say he would promptly repeat himself, until no one listened to anyone else. There were times when Jim could conduct an entire conversation with Collins and at the end not remember a word that either had said. It was a lonely time.

Suddenly he was aware Collins was talking. The subject? He waited until he caught the word *Seattle*.

"I'll show you around. I really know that town like nobody's business. Show you these girls I know, Swedes, Norwegians . . . you know, *blonde*." His eyes shone. "You'll be real popular. I was when I was your age. Oh, they all used to make a fuss over me. They used to roll dice to see

who was going to go with me. I was something, I guess.
You'll be the same way because they like young guys."

Jim was going to ask more but they were interrupted by
the steward, a tall lean Scot with no sense of humor.
"Willard, Collins, why're you not working?"

They fled.

On deck the wind was cold and sharp and full of spray.
Jim squinted in the wind as he made his way to the plump
woman's cabin.

He rapped on the door. "Come in."

His admirer wore a pink silk dressing gown that made her
look somewhat heavier than she actually was. She was cleaning her nails. A strong smell of salt and gardenia perfume
was in the air.

"Late today, aren't you?"

He mumbled agreement as he took the broom out of the
locker and began to sweep, quickly, self-consciously. She
watched him.

"Have you been a sailor long?"

He kept on cleaning. "No, ma'am."

"I didn't think you had. You're not very old, are you?"

"Twenty-one," he lied.

"Well, you had me fooled. You certainly look younger
than that." He wished she would stop talking. She went on.
"Whereabouts are you from?"

"Virginia."

"Really? I have relatives in Washington, D.C. You know
where that is, don't you?"

He was amused and irritated. She obviously thought him
simple. But he played the desired role. Nodding vaguely, he
opened the cabin door and swept the dirt out onto the
deck. "Where did you learn such housekeeping?" She was
endlessly inventive in her lust.

"Just came natural, I reckon," he said, mouth slightly ajar, idiot boy catching flies.

"Oh, really?" She was unaware that he was giving a performance. "I'll bet you never did that back home, did you?"

He said oh, yes, and began to make the bed, first brushing out the cigarette ashes. She continued to babble. "My friends in Washington say Virginia is lovely. I went to see the Blue Ridge Mountains once. You know where they are, don't you?"

This time he said no, and looked bewildered. She was informative. "I went all through those caverns underneath the mountains and they were very interesting, with all those stone things growing down and the others up. Is your mother alive? Are your family living in Virginia?"

He replied accurately.

"My, but your mother must be almost as old as I am," said the plump woman, making her first tentative move.

"I expect she is," he said evenly, taking the round on points.

"Oh." She was silent. He worked quickly; there were other cabins to be done.

"This is my first trip to Alaska," she said at last. "I have relatives in Anchorage. You've been to Anchorage, haven't you?" He nodded. "It's very civilized for Alaska, don't you think so? I mean I always thought of Alaska as being like the North Pole, all ice and snow. But Anchorage is just like a small town anywhere and they've got trees and beauty parlors, just like in the States. 'Outside,' they call the States. Isn't that a funny way to refer to the rest of the world? 'Outside'? I enjoyed myself very much visiting my relatives and so on. But you've traveled around a lot for someone so young, haven't you? I'll bet you've had some interesting experiences."

"Not so many." He finished making her bunk. When she saw he was ready to leave, she said quickly, "Oh, you're going to fix that porthole thing for me, aren't you? It keeps rattling all the time and I can't sleep at night."

He looked at the porthole cover and saw that a screw was loose. With his thumbnail he tightened it. "I don't think it'll bother you anymore," he said.

She got up, pulling her silk dressing gown tight at the throat, and joined him at the porthole.

"Aren't you clever! Why, I tried all night long last night to fix that thing and I couldn't."

He moved toward the door.

She spoke again, quickly, as though to prevent him from leaving by her talk. "My husband used to be good at fixing things. He's dead now, of course. He's been dead since 1930, but I've a son back home. He's much younger than you. He's just starting college. . . ." Jim felt as if he were being pushed to the edge of a cliff. With a son his age, she was trying to seduce him. Suddenly homesick, lost, he wanted to run away, to hide, to vanish. She was still talking as he opened the door and stepped out onto the wet, shining deck.

But he had no time to be lonely that evening. There was a party for the passengers, and it was a hard evening for the messboys.

The saloon was decorated with imitation holly and shedding branches of pine, which the steward had thoughtfully brought from Anchorage. Not until two in the morning did the last passenger leave the smoky saloon. Then the steward, red-faced and sweating, congratulated the messboys and wished them a Merry Christmas and told them that they could have their own party in the saloon.

Tired as they were, they managed to drink a good deal. Jim drank beer and Collins drank bourbon from a bottle given him by a young girl passenger. Then some of the men started to sing and soon everyone sang loudly, to show what a good time they were having. As Jim continued to drink beer, he felt a certain affection for the others. Together they would sail forever back and forth between Seattle and Anchorage until the ship sank or he died. Tears came to his eyes as he thought of this beautiful comradeship.

Collins was drunk now. "Come on, boy," he said, "stop being so gloomy."

Jim was hurt. "I feel fine," he said. "I'm not gloomy." Then he did become sad. "But I never thought that I'd be 'way up here last Christmas, be here on Christmas Day one year when a year ago I was home." He was not sure if this made sense but it had to be said.

"Well," said Collins happily, "I know I never thought I'd go to sea, back in Oregon where I lived. Old man was in the lumber business. Outside Eugene. Wanted me to go in the business, too, but I had to go places and so I went. But sometime, maybe, I'll go back. Settle down. Raise a family. . . ." His voice trailed off, bored with what he was saying. Then he stood up shakily and together they left the saloon. The night was cold and clear. The clouds were gone and across the shifting black water the peaks of Alaska were visible, defined by starlight.

Exhilarated, Jim breathed the cold air deeply.

"Some night," he said. But Collins was only interested in keeping his balance as they walked forward to the fo'c'sle.

The fo'c'sle was triangle-shaped with double-deck bunks and bare lightbulbs overhead, and heavy with the smell of too many men living in too small a place.

Jim had an upper bunk; Collins slept below him. Groan-

ing to show how tired he was, Collins sat down on his bunk.
"I'm wore out." He took off his shoes and stretched out. "I
can't wait to get to Seattle. You never been there, have
you?"

"Just passed through."

"Well, I'll show you 'round these dives I know. They
know me at all the waterfront places. And I'll get you a girl.
A real good one. What do you like?"

Jim was uncomfortable. "I don't know," he said. "Almost
anything."

"Hell, you got to be *particular* or you'll catch something
awful. Me, I never caught anything . . . yet." He touched
the wooden side of his bunk. "Get you a blonde, they're
best. Natural blondes, I mean. Swedes, that kind. You like
blondes?"

"Sure."

Collins pushed himself up on his elbow and looked at
Jim, suddenly alert. "Hey, I'll bet you're a virgin."

Jim flushed and couldn't think of anything to say; the
pause was enough.

"I'll be damned." Collins was delighted. "I never
thought I'd find a guy who was. Well, we'll be real careful
about the girl. How come you waited so long? You're eigh-
teen, aren't you?"

Jim was embarrassed. He cursed himself for not having
lied as all of them did about their affairs. "Oh, I don't
know," he said, trying to dismiss it. "There wasn't much
chance back home."

"I know just the girl for you. Name's Myra. Professional
but nice, and clean. She don't drink or smoke and because
she don't drink she takes care of herself. She won't give you
no dose. I'll get you and Myra together."

"I'd like to meet her," said Jim, and the beer he had
drunk made him excited at the idea. He dreamed occasion-

ally of women, but most often he dreamed of Bob, which disturbed him when he thought about it.

"I'll show you around," said Collins, undressing. "I'll show you one good time. Yes, sir, I know my way 'round."

II

IT WAS ALREADY EVENING when Collins and Jim left the ship. Collins wore a brown suit with red checks. Jim wore a gray suit that was already too tight in the shoulders. He was still growing. Neither wore a tie.

They took a streetcar to the theater district. Jim wanted to see a movie but Collins told him there was no time for that. "First we find us a room."

"I thought we were going to stay with these girls you been telling me about."

Collins gestured. "How do I know if they're in town, or if they ain't already booked for tonight? We'll get us a room; then we'll have a place to take whoever we find."

"You know a place like that?"

"I know a lot of places."

They found what they were looking for not far from the waterfront, in a street where the buildings were red brick and dingy and there were many bars, crowded with seamen prowling.

A bald wrinkled man sat behind a desk at the top of a long flight of flimsy steps. He was the proprietor of the Regent Hotel.

"We want a room for tonight," said Collins, and he put his lower jaw out to show that he meant what he said.

"Double room?"

Collins nodded and so did Jim.

The bald man said, "Pay in advance, two dollars apiece."

They paid in advance. "I don't want no loud noise or drinking or bringing women up here. You know the law, boys. You from a boat?"

"Yeah," said Collins, his jaw still out.

"I was a sailor myself once," said the bald man mildly. "But I don't follow the sea no more." He led them up two flights of steps, then down a dark, damp-smelling corridor to a small room. He turned on the light. The room was fairly clean, though the paint was flaking off the walls. A large iron bed was at the center of the room. A single window looked out upon the side of another brick building.

"Leave the key at the desk when you go out," said the bald man. He looked around the room a moment, pleased with what he saw. Then he left.

"Isn't this something?" Collins sat down on the bed and it creaked.

Jim was depressed. Though he had slept in worse places, he did occasionally wonder if he would ever again live in a room like his room in Virginia, a clean place with familiar walls.

"Come on," said Jim, turning to the door. "I'm hungry."

"Me too!" And Collins winked at Jim to show what he was hungry for.

They walked the dark streets, looking tough whenever they saw seamen, whistling boldly when any girls gave them the eye. It was good to be in Seattle on a clear winter night.

They stopped in front of a restaurant-bar. A neon sign announced spaghetti. "Here it is," said Collins. "This is the place."

"Where the girls are?" asked Jim.

"What else?" They went inside. The restaurant was large but only half-filled. A dark-haired waitress led them to a booth.

"So what've you got, honey?" Collins twinkled.

The waitress handed him a menu. "That's what I got," she said flatly and walked away.

"Stuck-up bitch," commented Collins, and Jim saw that his charm was not infallible. "Women shouldn't work anyway. Not with the Depression and all. They ought to stay home."

Jim looked around the restaurant. Red booths, brown walls, yellow-shaded lights: a cavern somewhere in hell.

After spaghetti, Collins belched and then announced, "We'll stay here awhile. Over there, at the bar. Then, if we don't see nothing we want, we'll go over to the Alhambra, this dance place where I know everybody."

The bar was not crowded. They ordered beer. "Swell place," said Collins, with a self-congratulatory air.

Jim agreed, adding somewhat maliciously, "Of course, they got hundreds of places like this back in New York." Collins had never been to the East Coast.

Collins frowned at his beer. "Well, I'll stick to little old Seattle." He took a drink of beer. "I'll bet," he said, making a point, "that *Hollywood* has got New York beat a mile." He knew that Jim had never been to Hollywood. "Yes," he went on, pleased at his own tactic, "I'll bet they got more pretty girls and crazy people and queers in L.A. than any other town."

"Maybe so."

Then the girl came up to the bar. Collins saw her first and nudged Jim. She was a slim girl with khaki hair, gray eyes, large features, large breasts. She sat down at the bar, smiling slightly. Red lips.

"What do you think of that?" murmured Collins.

"She's pretty."

"Real class, too," said Collins. "Probably works in an office." Apparently the bartender knew her because he said something to her in a low voice and they both laughed. He gave her a drink and she sat with it in her hand, watching the door.

"Here goes," said Collins, and went toward the men's room. On his way, he paused at the end of the bar. He looked at the girl, pretending to be puzzled by what he saw. He spoke to her. Jim couldn't hear what he said but he could see her frown, then smile. They talked a moment. She looked at Jim. She smiled again. Collins gestured for Jim to join them.

"Jim, this is Emily." They shook hands.

"It's a pleasure to meet you," said Emily, and her voice was husky and ladylike. Jim muttered a greeting.

"Don't mind him. He's real shy. We're on the same ship. We only got in today."

Emily was impressed, as she was supposed to be. "But you ought to be out on the town celebrating."

"We plan to. But the night is young, like they say."

"And so are we." Emily took a tiny sip of her drink. "Is this your first visit to Seattle?"

Collins shook his head. "I been in and out of Seattle most of my life. I know this old town backward and forward. In fact, I was thinking of showing Jim here some of the sights."

"Where are *you* from?" When Jim told her, she gave a little cry. "Oh, a Southerner! I love Southerners. They have such good manners. So you're from Virginia." She said Virginia as though it were Vur-gin-ee-ah. "But you haven't got much of an accent, have *you-all?*" Emily and Collins laughed at her mimetic skill.

Jim smiled. "No," he said, "I guess not."

"By the way"—Emily turned to Collins—"what sort of sights had you planned on seeing tonight?"

"Well, I thought maybe we'd go over to the Alhambra. . . ."

"Why, that's my very favorite place! My girl friend and I go there a lot to dance. You meet such nice people there. Not the rough gang you get in some places."

"Oh, you live with another girl?" Collins was on the scent.

Emily nodded. "We work in the same office and sometimes we go out on dates together. Tonight she was supposed to meet me here. Two boys she knows are coming into town (we think) and she was going to bring them here."

"Oh hell." Collins scowled and looked unhappy. "And here I was hoping maybe you and your friend could join Jim and me. You see the only girls I know in town happen to be away right now so I was hoping maybe . . ."

"Well," said Emily thoughtfully, "I *could* call her up and find out whether they are definitely going to come tonight or not and if they aren't . . . well, I think she would be *glad* to join us."

And so it was that Emily went to the back of the bar to telephone her roommate.

"How's that for operating?" asked Collins.

"Good." Jim was genuinely impressed. "Do you think her girl friend will really come?"

"Are you kidding?"

"She's pretty," said Jim, watching the blonde girl through the glass door of the telephone booth. He appreciated her handsomeness, but he was not moved by her in the way Collins was. He wanted very much to be excited by her. But it was no use, at least not while he was sober. It was very odd.

Emily joined them at the bar, red lips smiling. "My friend, Anne, is going to meet us in a few minutes at the Alhambra. She said that our two friends are *not* coming after all. You know, some people are so undependable that way. So, as I said to her, it's a lucky thing for us to have such a nice invitation from two boys just in town after such a long time at sea. Anne's just crazy about the sea. Once they gave an office party, a picnic out on the Sound, and Anne went sailing with one of the fellows and they could hardly get her back to shore she liked it so much."

"I guess," said Collins with a wink, "that Anne will be Jim's date. If that's all right."

Emily laughed and both of them watched her breasts shake. "Why, if it's all right with you, it is with me." And she looked at Collins, lips parted seductively. Then she turned to Jim. "I'm sure you'll like Anne. She's a lot of fun."

The Alhambra was a large dance hall on a side street, with a bright neon sign which flashed on and off above the mock-Moorish door.

Inside, the hall was crowded and dim. A small band played swing.

A gray-haired woman in a black evening dress led them to a table. Collins greeted her warmly. She looked at him blankly and left.

"Old friend of mine," said Collins. "I used to come in here a lot last year. She always remembers me."

A waiter came over and after a short discussion they ordered rye. Meanwhile, Emily made an unconscionable amount of conversation. "I expect to see Anne any minute now. She's the fastest dresser I've ever seen for a woman. And then we live just a few blocks from here."

"Yes?" Collins was alert.

"Just a few blocks," repeated Emily. Then: "Anne is really such a clever girl. Why, she even used to do modeling work."

"She must be real pretty," said Jim, forcing excitement.

Emily nodded. "Anne *is* good-looking. She's one of the

most popular girls in the office. She and I date together all the time and I'm sure that the fellow with me is always wishing he was with Anne." This was an excellent opening for Collins to protest. He protested. Emily continued. "She's younger than I am. She's twenty and I'm twenty-two. How old are you, Colly?"

"Twenty-five," lied Collins and he pulled his chair nearer hers.

Emily looked at Jim. "I'll bet you are not a day over twenty," she said with a grin.

Jim nodded solemnly. "That's right." Now that false ages had been established all around, the evening assumed direction.

Finally, Anne arrived. She was small and thin and she wore a brown dress. She looked about her uncertainly until she saw Emily. Then she hurried over, smiling, posing. Emily introduced everybody and then, as she was a little drunk, she introduced everybody a second time. This proved funny.

While Anne laughed, Jim decided that she was indeed pretty, though nearer thirty than twenty. Not that it made the slightest difference to him.

"And so you're Jim," said Anne after she had taken a drink and the excitement of her entrance was gone.

"That's right. Emily's been telling us a lot about you."

"Flattering, I hope?" At times Anne sounded like an English movie actress. Like her friend, she had a good deal of small talk.

"We work in an office in a department store. I file things and Emily types and does things like that. Are you from the South?"

He nodded and she made up a funny sentence with "you-all" in it and everybody laughed and then Emily and Collins got up from the table and announced that they were going to dance. So Jim invited Anne and all four of them went out onto the dance floor. Jim made an effort to dance well. There were so many things to be proved this evening.

Anne pressed close to him, her cheek against his; he could smell powder and soap and perfume. Once he looked down at her and saw that her eyes were closed.

Collins came by with Emily. "Hey, Jim," he said. Anne opened her eyes and Jim moved a few inches away from her.

"Yes?" said Jim.

"Emily here's suggested we go over to their place for a while. They've got liquor over there and a radio and we can dance where it won't be so crowded."

"That's a good idea, Emily," said Anne brightly.

They went back to their table, paid the check, gathered coats, and left the Alhambra. Though the night was cold, Jim was sweating from whiskey.

In a side street they stopped before a small apartment house. Emily opened the door. At the top of two flights of clean and carpeted stairs, Emily showed them into an apartment consisting of a sitting room, a small kitchen, and a bedroom. The door to the bedroom was open and Jim could see twin beds inside.

"Home," announced Emily, turning on the radio while Anne disappeared into the kitchen, returning a moment later with a bottle of rye and some glasses. "Get some ice, will you, Emily?"

Emily went into the kitchen, followed by Collins. Anne put the glasses down on the table and Jim stood beside her, awkward, unsure of himself.

"Let's dance," she said, when she had arranged the glasses on a table. He held her away from him, but she pressed close. He was ill at ease. He wanted desperately to be carried away by the music and the whiskey and this girl, but all he could think of was the flecks of dandruff in her hair.

He heard a laugh from the kitchen. Then Collins and Emily came into the sitting room. Both were flushed and Collins's eyes were bright. Emily put a bowl of ice cubes on the table and Collins produced a bottle of soda water.

"Let's all have a drink," said Emily. They all had a drink. Collins proposed a toast to Emily and she graciously proposed one to him. Jim and Anne toasted each other. Jim was drunk now. His eyes refused to focus. Everything was suddenly warm and cozy and intimate. Boldly he put his arm around Anne and they sat down on a couch, side by side, and watched Collins and Emily dance.

"You really dance well," said Anne. "You must've taken lessons. I never took any lessons but I picked up a lot from the girls I knew in school. I went to a secretarial school and we used to have a lot of dances. I enjoyed them so much. And that's where I learned how to dance."

He wanted to keep her talking. "Did you always live in Seattle?"

She scowled to show that this was a question which troubled her. "Yes, I've always lived here but I don't like it. You see, I want to travel. I've *always* wanted to travel. That's why I envy you men on ships, you get to travel so much and see so many things."

"Where would you like to go?" As Jim held her, he was pleasurably astonished at his own bravery. She moved close to him.

"Everywhere," she said. "But mainly I want to see Southern California. I want to go to Hollywood. You know, I think I'd like to be in the movies." She said this in a low voice, confidingly.

"I guess a lot of people do." Jim had read a few movie magazines and he had been impressed by the difficulties movie stars encountered in becoming movie stars.

"I know," said Anne. "But I think I'm different. No,

really. I'm serious. I think I'm going to be famous. Why, even when I was younger and saw people like Jean Harlow on the silver screen I knew that would be me one day. But for now I got to work in an office and I don't know when I'll be able to get to Hollywood. But I'll get there someday. I just know it."

"You've certainly got ambition."

"Oh, I've got plenty of that! Just think what it'd be like to wear all those pretty clothes and have men with mustaches and tweed suits take me out to eat in those expensive places with palm trees." She stared into space, her mouth open with longing for this other life.

Jim muttered soothing things, aware that Collins and Emily had disappeared. The door to the bedroom was still open, and he could see Collins in his shorts approaching Emily, who lay naked on one of the beds. Emily giggled. Jim looked away, blushing.

"What's the matter?" Anne abandoned her Hollywood vision. Then she saw what was happening in the bedroom. She giggled, an echo of Emily.

"You're only young once," she said. Jim looked at her and saw that her eyes were bright, shiny, bestial. He had seen the same look in Collins's eyes, in Emily's eyes, yet not in Bob's eyes. He was repelled. But Anne, unaware of his response, put her face so close to his that he could smell the whiskey on her breath. "My, but they're having fun!" Her body was against him now and he could feel the rapid pounding of her heart.

"I'll bet they're having a good time," she repeated. "You're only young once, that's what I say." She kissed him. It was a wet and tongue-involving kiss. He pulled away. Aware of his withdrawal, she started to cry. "I used to be in love, too," she said, missing the point. Between small actress sobs, she said that she understood the way he felt and she knew that what she was doing was terribly bad but she was lonely, without anyone to care for her, and God knows they were only young once.

He made himself kiss her, his mind full of memories and half-forgotten fears. With an effort of will, he tried to melt the fear in his stomach. Gradually, desire began. He was startled but pleased. Soon he would be ready. But suddenly she stood up and said brightly, "I better take my dress off. Don't want to get it rumpled."

She went into the bedroom. He followed her to the door and stood watching Collins and Emily on the bed. Neither of them seemed to care if they were observed or not. They were involved in the intricate act of becoming one. Fascinated, Jim watched them. They made primitive noises and writhed blindly, according to the mindless ritual of the sexes. Jim was frightened, unready for this.

Anne appeared, and posed for him without her clothes. He stared, fascinated. He had never seen a naked woman before. She walked toward him. She put out her arms. Involuntarily, he backed away.

"Come on in, Jimmy," she said and her voice was high-pitched and artificial. He hated her then. He hated her passionately. This was not what he wanted.

"I got to go," he said. He went into the sitting room. She followed him and he found himself staring at her again and this time he compared her with Bob, and found her wanting. He no longer cared whether or not he was different from other people. He hated this woman and her body.

"What's the matter? What did I do wrong?"

"I got to go." He couldn't say anything else. She started to cry. Quickly he went to the door and opened it. Just as he left, he heard Collins shout to Anne, "Let the queer go! I got enough for two."

Jim walked a long time in the cold night and wondered

why he had failed so completely in what he had wanted to do. He was not what Collins had called him. He was certain of that. Yet why? At the moment when what should have happened was about to happen, the image of Bob had come between him and the girl, rendering the act obscene and impossible. What to do? He would not exorcise the ghost of Bob even if he could. Yet he realized that it would be a difficult matter to live in a world of men and women without participating in their ancient and necessary duet. Was he able to participate? Yes, he decided, under other circumstances. In any case, the word Collins had shouted after him was hardly apt. It couldn't be. It was too monstrous. Yet because it had been said, he could never see Collins again. He would jump ship and go . . . where? He looked down the dark empty street, searching for a sign. Just opposite him was a movie house. "*Yesterday's Magic,* starring Ronald Shaw," proclaimed the marquee in unlit lightbulbs. He thought of Hollywood, recalling Anne's voice droning on wistfully about the movies. That did it. At least he would get there before she did. Obscurely pleased at this small vengeance, he returned to the hotel.

The bald-headed man was still behind the desk. "You're a sailor. I can tell. Me, I was a sailor but I don't follow the sea no more. No, no more of that for me." Jim went to his room and tried to sleep, tried to forget what Collins had called him. He slept and he forgot.

CHAPTER
4

I

OTTO SCHILLING WAS HALF-AUSTRIAN and half-Polish. He was blond with a brick-red face, much lined from weather. He was tennis instructor at the Garden Hotel in Beverly Hills.

"You were a sailor, yes?" Otto's accent was thick, though he had been in America half his life.

"Yes, sir." Jim was nervous. He needed this job.

"When did you leave ship?"

"Last December."

Otto looked thoughtfully out the window at his kingdom, the eight clay courts which adjoined the hotel pool.

"That was six months ago. You have been in Los Angeles since then?"

"Yes, sir."

"You have been what?"

"Working in a garage mostly."

"But you play tennis, yes?"

"Yes, sir. I used to play back home at school."

"How old are you?"

"Nineteen."

"You think you know enough to help around here? Roll courts, be ball boy, string rackets . . . you can do this?"

"Yes, sir. I talked to the guy who was here before and he told me what the work was and I know I can do it."

Otto Schilling nodded. "I take you on trial. That boy was here before was lazy. You better not be lazy. You get twenty-five a week, but I make you work hard for all that money. If you're any good, you help me give lessons. Maybe I let *you* give lessons, if you play good. You play good?" His wide blue eyes looked at Jim.

"I was pretty good," said Jim, trying to sound both modest and informative.

Otto nodded approvingly. He did not share the American passion for modesty. When he had been singles champion of Austria, there were those who had thought him conceited. But why not? He had been a great player. "You will live in the hotel," he said finally. "Go see Mr. Kirkland, the manager. I call him on the phone now. You start in the morning, seven-thirty o'clock. I tell you what to do. Maybe I play with you and see what you know. Go on now."

Jim murmured "Thank you" and left the tennis house. On his right was a large swimming pool edged with imported beach. Prosperous-looking men and women sat beneath umbrellas, while several young girls were photographed by a sinister-looking cameraman. Jim wondered if the girls were movie stars, and if so, who they were. But they all looked alike, with white teeth, bleached hair, slim brown bodies. He recognized no one.

Jim climbed the steps to the Garden Hotel, a large,

rambling, white stucco building set among palm trees. After six months of uncomfortable rooming houses, he was delighted at the thought of living here, if only temporarily. He was quite used by now to being transient. He took it for granted that his traveling would not end until he found Bob. Then they would work out some sort of life together, though precisely what that life would be he left deliberately vague. Meanwhile, he took what work he could find, and lived happily in the present. Except for the golden image of Bob beside the river on that sunshine day, he was without history. In memory, his father was a dim blur; his mother, too; both gray, shadowy. The sea was dark and vaguest of all. Everything forgotten except Collins and the two girls in their Seattle apartment. Only that night was vivid in his memory. With an effort, he tried not to think of it as he hurried up the steps to the Garden Hotel.

Mr. Kirkland's office was large and modern and looked much more expensive than it actually was. So did Mr. Kirkland. He was a short man whose real name was probably not Kirkland. He affected a British accent, while his clothes and manner were exquisite and discreet, except for the large diamond he wore on the little finger of his left hand, an outward and visible sign of sudden rise and of unfamiliar affluence.

"Willard?" the voice was sharp.

"Yes, sir. Mr. Schilling sent me to you."

"You're going to be ball boy, I understand." Mr. Kirkland pronounced the title as though it were an accolade. "As such, you will be paid twenty-five dollars a week. Quite a large amount for a young boy, but I trust you will work for it to the best of your ability." Jim recognized a speech that had been made before. "We here at the Garden Hotel like to think of ourselves as a family, in which each one must do his part, from myself"—he smiled tightly—"on down."

He looked at Jim. "You start work as of tomorrow morning. I suppose you gave your references to Mr. Schilling. Ask the housekeeper in the servants' wing to assign you a room." With a nod, Mr. Kirkland ended the interview and Jim departed.

The lobby of the hotel was large with square marble pillars, which pretended to hold up the lozenge-patterned ceiling. The floor was carpeted in royal red. Behind a plywood desk simulating mahogany, clerks in formal clothes received guests, simulating welcome. Bellboys in livery lounged on a bench at the front door, waiting to carry bags and run errands. The lobby was usually a busy place, for there was always someone arriving or departing. Jim found the magnificence awesome and the bored air of the bellboys infinitely sophisticated. Perhaps one day he would be as casual.

Jim crossed the lobby, conscious of his shabby suitcase. He approached one of the bellboys and asked uncertainly, "How do I get to the employees' wing?"

The young man looked at him with slow boredom. Then he yawned and stretched. "I'll take you back." They went from the lobby to the famous tropical garden, which gave the hotel its name. Dazzled by color, Jim followed his guide through the artificial jungle.

"What's your job?"

Jim told him.

"An outdoor boy! So where you from?"

Jim decided to be impressive. "Nowhere. I been to sea."

The young man was respectful but inquiring. "To sea *where?*"

Jim was offhand. "Caribbean, Pacific, Bering Sea, all over. I been around."

"I guess you have. So what're you doing here?"

Jim shrugged. "Killing time. What else?"

The young man nodded and thoughtfully scratched one of a number of pimples.

Jim was assigned a small room overlooking the parking lot. The housekeeper was pleasant and the bellboy promised to show him the ropes. The thing was done. He now had a small place in the world of others.

In Southern California September was not much different from any other month. The weather was clear and bright and there was no rain. According to the newspapers there was a war in Europe, but Jim was not quite sure what it was all about. Apparently there was a man named Hitler who was German. He had a mustache and comedians were always imitating him. At every party someone was bound to give an imitation of Hitler making a speech. Then there was an Englishman with a somewhat larger mustache and of course there was Mussolini but he didn't seem to be in the war. For a while it was very exciting, and there were daily headlines. But toward the end of September Jim lost interest in the war because there had been no battles. Also, his days were now occupied teaching tennis to rich men and women who were not very interested in the war either.

Schilling liked Jim, and, after they had played together several times, he allowed him to instruct. He also encouraged him to go into tournaments, but Jim was satisfied to continue as he was. The life was easy and healthy. He gained weight; his body thickened with muscle. He was popular with the people who used the courts, particularly the young girls who lived in the hotel. They flirted with him, and he always responded politely, if evasively, which made them think him sensitive as well as handsome.

He was now used to the sight of famous actors and actresses playing tennis and sunning themselves beside the pool. In fact, one brilliant old actress (almost forty) took lessons from him every day, swearing obscenely whenever she made a bad shot. He thought her most impressive.

Jim had also begun a social life. Several times he had gone on parties with the bellhops. Most of them wanted to be actors, which explained the somewhat detached air with which they did their various jobs around the hotel. Several took a fancy to Jim because he didn't want to become an actor; also, he seemed sincerely to admire them. Jim was not without social guile. Yet his new companions puzzled him. Their conversation was often cryptic, their eyes quick-moving, searching. Ill at ease with outsiders, they were quarrelsome with one another. The one thing they had in common was the desire to move in splendor through the lives of others, to live forever grandly, and not to die.

They had many rich friends who gave parties, consisting largely of middle-aged women, widowed or divorced, and plump men with unpleasant habits when drunk. The women particularly took a fancy to Jim and he was often told that he was a "real person" and not like the others, whatever that meant. The plump men were also nice to him but, when through ignorance he did not respond to the suggestive ritual of their conversation, they left him alone.

Otto Schilling warned Jim about the bellhops. He explained that since they were not normal young men, they would try to corrupt him. Otto was stern as he explained these matters to Jim, who managed to look so shocked and unbelieving (he *was* surprised) that Otto spared him the full explanation of what he meant.

Jim went through several stages after his discovery that there were indeed many men who liked other men. His first reaction was disgust and alarm. He scrutinized everyone carefully. Was he one? After a while, he could identify the obvious ones by their tight, self-conscious manner, particularly when they moved, neck and shoulders rigid. After a time, as the young men grew used to Jim, they would talk frankly about themselves. Finally, one tried to seduce him. Jim was quite unnerved, and violent in his refusal. Yet afterward he continued to go to their parties, if only to be able to experience again the pleasure of saying no.

Late one afternoon, a bellhop named Leaper entered the tennis house just as Jim was finishing his shower. Leaper peered into the shower room. "Hey, Jim."

Jim rubbed soap out of his eyes. "Hi!" Though Leaper was one of those he had refused, they had remained on good terms.

"You want to go to a party?"

"Where?" Jim turned off the shower, picked up his towel, and joined Leaper in the locker room. As he dried himself, he knew that he was being examined with passionate interest. He was more amused than irritated.

"At Ronald Shaw's. In Beverly."

Jim was surprised. "The movie actor?"

"The very same, and they say he is quite *sympathetic.*" Leaper made a feminine gesture. "He asked a friend of mine to collect some beauties so I thought of you. Of course you may be the only straight guy there, but then you can never tell, there might be some girl with red hair hanging on to the fringes." Jim had developed a mythical reputation for liking girls with red hair. Leaper chattered happily about Ronald Shaw while Jim dressed.

"It's really something to go to one of Shaw's parties. He's an honest-to-God Movie Star, with all the girls everywhere mad for him! That's a joke, isn't it? Why, when I worked in a picture with him at Metro . . ." Like most of the bellhops, Leaper had done extra work in the movies and he spoke often of stars he had "worked with." "These Girl Scouts came around to give him some sort of prize and he said: 'Will you please take these pubescent monsters and lay them end to end on the back lot.' Of course they covered it all up, just like the time he was knocked down in a bar at Santa Monica by this Marine from Pendleton. Oh, that guy is *something*!"

"He's pretty young, isn't he?" Jim parted his wet hair in the mirror.

"Thirty, maybe. You can't tell about those guys. Anyway, you better be warned, he'll make a pass at you, which I bet you wouldn't mind one bit."

"Just let him try," growled Jim into the mirror, aware that his suntanned face made him resemble a South Sea–movie islander. "Sure I'll come," he said, ready for adventure.

II

AT THIRTY-FIVE, RONALD SHAW was disturbingly handsome, with features of such ordinariness that they were, paradoxically, unique. Dark curly hair tumbled over a classic low forehead to give him a look often described as "impish" by admirers, "Neanderthal" by detractors. With his light blue eyes, he seemed typically "black Irish," a type which occurs most often among Jews. Ronald Shaw had been born George Cohen. At one point he had thought that to be taken for George M. Cohan might be rewarding, but it was not, and so George Cohen became Ronald Shaw, a handsome, fiery young Irishman whose films made money. George Cohen of Baltimore had been very poor but now that Ronald Shaw was wealthy neither was going to be poor again. Shaw was notoriously mean, except with his mother in Baltimore. As every reader of movie magazines knew, his mother was his "best girl" and the reason that he was still a bachelor, which was exactly right, as any Freudian would agree.

Although Shaw had been a star for five years, he had never bought a house in Hollywood. He preferred to rent large impersonal houses where he could give parties for young men behind thick walls and an elaborate burglar-alarm system. In his way, he was discreet. Yet everyone in the homosexual world knew that he was one of them. Naturally there were rumors about other actors, but where in other cases there was often some vestigial doubt in the minds of even the most passionate apologists for Socratic vice, there was none in Shaw's case. He was always mentioned by the great fraternity with pride, envy, lust. Fortunately, the women of America remained in ignorance, regarding him as a satisfying love object, unattainable but useful as a companion in dreams, the boy-man of advertising come alive thirty times life-size upon the screen.

Ronald Shaw had it made, and since he was nothing if not human, he found most human relationships disappointing. His sexual partners were selected for a combination of physical beauty and hard masculinity. Each affair began as though the creation of the world was to be reenacted, and each usually ended in less time than it took the Old Testament Creator to put up the sky. No one could please Shaw for very long. If a boy came to love him (and to disregard the legend) Shaw was affronted and endangered; yet if a lover continued to be dazzled by the idea of him, he soon grew bored. Nevertheless, Shaw was a happy man, and if he had not been told about romantic love, it would never have occurred to him to take coupling seriously.

Jim was much impressed by the magnificence of Shaw's house. An interior decorator had done it for nothing; unfortunately, the affair had ended before the bedrooms were done. Nevertheless, the downstairs was a success, a riot of Spanish baroque with a huge drawing room whose windows looked down upon Los Angeles, glittering to the west. Over a cavernous fireplace hung a portrait of Ronald Shaw, half again as large as life. The original of this glamorous work of art stood at the center of the room, graciously directing the party's traffic. It was an odd group. For one thing, there were three times as many men as women. Jim recognized several character actors: Ronald Shaw needed only the flimsiest support. The women were all elegant, with high voices, large jewels, towering befeathered hats. They were not, Jim was assured by the knowing Leaper, lesbians. They had simply passed the age of being able to attract normal men and so, still craving attention, they were drawn into the world of hairdressers and couturiers. Here they could gossip and make stage love and avoid boredom, if not despair.

"Isn't this swell?" murmured Leaper, in his awe forgetting his role as sophisticate and guide.

Jim nodded. "Where's Ronald Shaw?"

Leaper pointed to the center of the room. At first, Jim was disappointed. Shaw was smaller than he had expected. But he was handsome, there was no denying that. In contrast to the others, he wore a dark suit, which gave his slim figure dignity. At the moment he was surrounded by women. The young men were more circumspect; they held to the periphery of the party, waiting.

"You better meet him," said Leaper.

They crossed to the group of women and waited until Shaw had finished telling a story. Then, during the sharp, loud laughter, Leaper said hurriedly, "You remember me, Mr. Shaw, don't you?" Shaw looked blank but Leaper kept right on talking. "It was Mr. Ridgeway who asked me to come tonight, and I brought this friend of mine with me, Jim Willard. He's real keen to meet you. . . ."

Ronald Shaw smiled at Jim. "How do you do?" His hand was cool and hard.

"I . . . like you in the movies," said Jim, to Leaper's horror. This was impossibly bad form. With movie stars, one was supposed to appear unimpressed.

But admiration never offended Ronald Shaw. He grinned, showing white teeth. "That's nice of you to say so. Come on, let's get you a drink." Gracefully, Shaw extricated himself from the women and together they crossed to the far end of the room.

Acutely embarrassed, Jim was conscious of many eyes watching him. But Shaw was serenely at ease as he stopped a waiter and took a glass from the tray. "I hope you like martinis."

"Well, I don't drink very much."

"Neither do I." Shaw's voice was low and confiding, as if the only person in the world whose company and good opinion he sought was the bedazzled Jim. And though he asked only the usual questions, his warm voice made those familiar phrases sound significant, even the inevitable "Are you an actor?"

Jim quickly told him what he was.

Shaw grinned. "An athlete! Well. . . . You look too young to be an instructor." They were standing now at one of the large windows. Out of the corner of his eye, Jim noticed that his fellow guests were preparing to close in on Shaw and recapture him. They did not have much time. Shaw sensed this, too. "What's your name again?" Jim told him. "You must," said Shaw, looking thoughtfully down at the city, "come see me someday. When are you free?"

"I'm not working Thursday afternoon," said Jim, startled at the speed of his own response.

"Then why don't you drop by here Thursday. If I'm still shooting, you can swim until I get back. I'm usually through at five."

"Sure. I'd like to." Jim felt his stomach contract with fear and expectancy.

"See you Thursday." Then Ronald Shaw, with a distant polite nod calculated to deceive his audience, allowed the young men to surround him.

Leaper joined Jim. "Well, you're in." His eyes glittered. "He fell for you like a ton of—"

"Shut up, will you?" Jim turned away angrily.

"Don't con me. You hooked him. Everybody saw you. They want to know who you are. So I've been telling them you're straight as a die, which just makes their mouths water all the more. You're a hit, boy. Look at them all staring at you." Jim looked but caught no one staring. "So what did Shaw talk to you about?"

"Nothing."

"Oh, sure! Well, you better put out this time. He can do a lot for you."

"Sorry, I got no plans to shack up with him. Or anybody else."

Leaper looked at him with genuine surprise. "So maybe you're not queer, but *this* is an exception. Why, this is something people dream about. You could make a fortune out of him."

Jim laughed and moved away. He tried to appear relaxed and at ease, but he was neither. Soon he would have to make a decision, on Thursday to be precise. What to do? Mechanically he moved through the evening, his heart pounding. When it came time to say good-bye, Shaw smiled and winked. Blushing, Jim turned away. He said not a word to Leaper as they rode home in the bus.

III

JIM WILLARD'S EROTIC LIFE took place almost entirely in dreams. Until that day with Bob beside the river, he had dreamed of women as often as of men, and there had seemed no set boundary between the two. But since that summer day, Bob was the constant dream-lover, and girls no longer intruded upon their perfect masculine idyll. He was aware that what he dreamed of was not what normal men dreamed of. But at the same time he made no connection between what he and Bob had done and what his new acquaintances did. Too many of them behaved like women. Often after he had been among them, he would study himself in a mirror to see if there was any trace of the woman in his face or manner; and he was always pleased that there was not. Finally, he decided that he was unique. He was the only one who had done what he had done and felt the way he did. Even the elegant, long-haired youths all agreed that he was probably not one of them. Nevertheless, women expected him to make love to them, and when he didn't (he could never quite explain to himself *why* he didn't) they felt that it was they who were lacking, not he. None suspected that he dreamed every night of a tall boy by a river. Yet as Jim got more and more involved in Leaper's world, he found himself fascinated by the stories they told of their affairs with one another. He could not imagine himself doing the things they said they did. Yet he wanted to know about them, if only out of a morbid desire to discover how what had been so natural and complete for him could be so perfectly corrupted by these strange womanish creatures.

In a mood of indecision, Jim went to see Ronald Shaw, and what he suspected would happen did happen. He allowed himself to be seduced, impressed by Shaw's fame and physical beauty. The act was familiar except that this time he was passive, too shy to be the aggressor. With Bob he had taken the initiative, but then that was a different occasion and a more important time.

The affair began. Shaw was in love, or at least he talked of love, and how they would spend the rest of their lives together ("like those two ancient Greeks—you know the ones, Achilles and so-and-so—who were such famous lovers"). Not that there was to be any publicity. Hollywood was a merciless place and they would have to be extremely discreet. But for those who did know about them, they would be worshiped as a dazzling couple, two perfect youths, reenacting boyhood dreams behind the stucco walls of the house on Mulholland Drive.

Although Jim was flattered by Shaw's protestations of love, the older man's body did not excite him. Jim was oddly reluctant to touch a mature man's flesh, no matter how handsome he was. Apparently only those his own age had the power to attract him. Yet when he shut his eyes, he enjoyed himself, for then he would think of Bob. And so the affair began, or the "relationship," as those who had undergone analysis would say. It was a new experience for Jim and not entirely a pleasant one.

The first skirmish with the world occurred when Jim told Otto Schilling that he was going away.

Schilling was surprised. "I don't understand," he said. "I don't understand why you want to leave here. You get more pay somewhere else?"

Jim nodded.

Schilling looked at him sharply. "Where? How?"

Jim was uncomfortable. "Well, you see, Ronald Shaw, the actor, and these other people" (he added vaguely) "want me to teach, you know, on their courts, and so I said I would."

"Where will you live?"

Jim could feel the sweat trickling down his side. "I'll stay at Shaw's place."

Schilling nodded grimly and Jim kicked himself for not having lied. Everyone knew about Shaw. Jim felt ashamed. "I didn't think you were like that," said Schilling slowly. "I am sorry for you. There is nothing wrong with seeing a person like Ronald Shaw, there is nothing so wrong with being that way, but to be a kept boy, ah, *that* is bad."

Jim wiped his forehead with the back of his hand. "Is there anything you want me to do before I go?"

"No," said Schilling wearily. "Tell Mr. Kirkland you're leaving. That's all." He turned away.

Shaken, Jim went to his room and started to pack. Leaper joined him. "Congratulations!" he exclaimed. "Beginner's luck, you can't beat it."

"What're you talking about?" Jim packed furiously.

"Come off it. It's the talk of the circuit how you're going to live with Ronald Shaw! So what's he like?"

"I don't know." Jim felt his facade of normality crumbling.

"So what're you going to be, his cook?"

"I'm going to teach him tennis." This sounded idiotic even to his own ears. Leaper brayed contempt. But Jim stuck doggedly to his story, explaining how Shaw was to pay him fifty dollars a week, which was true.

"Ask me over sometime," said Leaper as Jim finished packing. "We could play doubles."

Jim merely glared. Yet in all of this one thing surprised him: Leaper, believing that Jim was heterosexual, took it for granted that any normal boy would live with a famous actor, given the chance. In Leaper's world all men were whores and all whores were bisexual.

Shaw was sitting beside the swimming pool when Jim arrived. The swimming pool was set like a navel in a red-brick terrace flanked by two bathhouses resembling the turreted pavilions of a medieval knight. Shaw waved as Jim approached.

"Did you make a clean break?" The deep voice was mocking.

"Clean enough. I told Schilling I was going to teach you and some other people tennis."

"You mentioned me?"

"Yes. I wish I hadn't. I'm sorry. Because he knew exactly what was going on. He didn't say much but I felt like dirt."

Shaw sighed. "I don't know how the hell they know so much about me. It's the damnedest thing." Like most homosexuals, Shaw was astonished that anyone saw through his mask. "I guess it's because so many people are so bloody jealous of me." Shaw sounded both sad and proud. "Because everyone knows who I am and because I make a lot of money, they all think I must be terribly happy, which they resent and which isn't so. Funny, isn't it? I've had all the things I ever wanted and I'm not . . . well, it's an awful feeling not having anybody to be close to. Oh, I tried to get my mother to come out here but she won't leave Baltimore. So here I am, all alone, like the song says. At least until now." He gave a flashing smile. Jim smiled back, in spite of himself. He couldn't help thinking that the man did have everything, and if he hadn't found a lover by now it was doubtless his own fault.

Jim unbuttoned his shirt. The day was warm and the sun was pleasant. He sat very still, trying not to contemplate the sadness of the life of Ronald Shaw. But Shaw was persistent. "You know," he said, "I don't think I've ever known anyone like you. Somebody so natural and . . . well, unscheming. I also didn't think you could be made. You don't seem the type." Jim was pleased to hear this, faith in his own manhood momentarily restored. Shaw grinned. "But I'm glad things turned out the way they did."

Jim smiled, too. "So am I."

"I hate those others, those lousy queens." Shaw lifted one shoulder and gave a curiously feminine shake to his body, mocking in a single gesture the entire legion.

"They're OK, some of them."

"I'm not talking about them as people," said Shaw. "I mean for sex. If a man likes men, he wants a man, and if he likes women, he wants a woman, so who wants a freak who's neither? It's a mystery to me." Shaw yawned. "Maybe I ought to be psychoanalyzed."

"Why?"

Shaw examined his biceps muscles critically: his appearance was his livelihood. "I don't know. Sometimes I . . ." But he did not pursue the thought. The arms went slack. "Bunch of fakes, every last one of them, telling you stuff you already know. No, what matters is being tough. You *got* to be tough in this world. There's no place for the weak, like Mamma used to say. She was right, too. That's how I got where I am, being tough and not feeling sorry for myself."

Jim was impressed by the sternness of this speech. He was also reminded of his own situation. "That's OK for you," he said, "this being tough. You had talent. You knew what you wanted. But what about me? I'm just a better-than-average tennis player. So what do *I* do? Toughness isn't going to help me play any better."

Shaw looked at him, obviously making an effort to

consider the case. "Well, I don't know." The beautiful eyes went slightly out of focus. "Would you . . . uh, like to act?"

Jim shrugged. "Me? Why?"

"Well, that's not what I'd call burning ambition. No, you've got to *want* this thing so much it hurts." And Shaw resumed the monologue which pleased him most, the chronicle of his own rise in the world, aided by no one except Mamma. Within the circle of his own self-love, Shaw was content, and Jim did not in the least resent being at the periphery of that self-absorption. Jim accepted Shaw completely and uncritically. After all, their affair was but a temporary halt on a long voyage whose terminus was Bob.

When Shaw had finished his hymn to achievement, Jim said, with an admiration not entirely false, "I guess I haven't got it," he said. "I don't want anything that bad."

Shaw fondled the vertical line of dark hair on his own chest. "We could certainly get you work as an extra. Then— who knows?"

"Who knows?" Jim rose and stretched. Shaw watched him, pleased and aroused.

"Put your bathing trunks on," he said, and he led Jim into the knight's pavilion.

IV

Two months passed peacefully. Jim enjoyed the large house with its rooms like movie sets. On the days when Shaw was at the studio, Jim would play tennis with various friends who wanted to meet Shaw's new lover as well as improve their backhand. Jim was agreeably surprised to find himself something of a celebrity, at least in this one world, and the interest he inspired compensated somewhat for the shame he had felt with Schilling.

Jim enjoyed Shaw's parties and he quickly made himself useful. He learned how to cope with drunks, mix drinks, and discreetly cue Shaw if there was a story he wanted to tell. Jim was much impressed by the beautifully dressed people who drank heavily and talked incessantly of their sex life. Their harsh candor both shocked and pleased him. They feared nothing, at least behind the high stucco walls of Shaw's estate.

Jim found Shaw not only an agreeable companion but, more important, informative. He showed him the secret Hollywood where, so it was said, nearly all the leading men were homosexual and those few who were not were under constant surveillance. A number of women acted as outriders to the beautiful legion, and they were often called upon to be public escorts. They were known as "beards." But they were not always reliable. One evening a drunken outrider tried to make love to Shaw and, when he pushed her away, she shouted obscenities at everyone present; then she was led away and no one ever saw her again.

For purposes of publicity, Shaw appeared regularly at nightclubs with girls, often rising actresses. He did this to satisfy the head of the studio, a nervous businessman whose nightmare was that scandal might end the career of his hottest property.

Jim liked Shaw, though he never believed him when, together at night, he would tell Jim how much he loved him. For one thing, the speeches flowed so easily that even the inexperienced Jim recognized that the actor was play-acting. Nor was Jim disturbed. He was not in love with Shaw, nor did he pretend to be. For one thing, the idea of being in love with a man was both ludicrous and unnatural; at the most a man might find his twin, like Bob, but that was rare and something else again.

One day, Shaw took Jim to the studio. As a rule they

never went out in public together, but today Shaw thought it time Jim saw him work.

The studio was an immense enclosure of white sound-stages, resembling mammoth garages. As Shaw drove through the studio gate, he was saluted respectfully by the gateman, while a pack of girls gave shrieks of recognition and waved autograph books at him.

Beyond the gate was another world, peopled with costumed extras, executives, technicians, laborers. Twenty films were being made simultaneously. Nothing else on earth mattered here.

They parked in front of a bungalow framed by hibiscus.

"My dressing room." Shaw was already beginning to get businesslike. Inside, stretched on a sofa, was a small bald man.

"Baby, you're late. I got here half an hour ago, like we agreed. And so far I've read *Variety*, the *Reporter*, and even the script."

"I'm sorry, Cy." Shaw introduced Jim to the man on the sofa. "Cy's directing my picture."

"If that's what you can call what I'm doing in this miserable place." Cy moaned. "Why did I ever leave New York? Why didn't I stay with the Group Theater?"

"Because they didn't want you, baby." Shaw grinned as he shed his jacket.

"There he stands. Pound for pound, the worst actor in America." Cy turned to Jim. "All he's got is that adorable smile and those obscene pectorals . . . or pector*i*als, as they say out here."

"Jealous, baby?" Shaw stripped to his shorts and flexed his celebrated pectorals. Cy groaned with disgust and shut his eyes.

"I can't stand it!" He pointed to a door. "Get your costume on. Makeup's been waiting since seven."

Shaw stepped into the next room, leaving the door ajar. "So what's the schedule?"

"A new scene, that's what. The writers were at it all night. They wrote this wonderful new scene on a menu at the Cotton Club. You'll love it."

"Am I terribly brave?"

"What else? They've given you a stiff upper lip, a tight sphincter . . . *everything*."

"A tight what?"

"I'll say one thing, if they ever educated one of you dopes it'd be the end of the American Dream. You agree, baby?" Cy gave Jim a sharp look.

"Sure," said Jim.

"Sure," mimicked Cy. "What am I doing here?" he asked the ceiling.

"Making fifteen hundred a week" came Shaw's voice from the next room, "and that's nothing for a good director, but for you . . ."

"Is this my reward for coming here to try and help you with this crucial new scene so that when you face the Big Brownie you'll know what you're doing? Yes, this is my reward, and you'll just wing the words like always, and another moneymaking bagel will drop into the laps of the American moviegoers. I guess you want to be an actor, too?" Again the sharp eyes turned to Jim.

"Well . . ."

"Well, *of course*! Where else in the world can a guy with no brain and no talent get to be rich and famous all because . . ."

Shaw entered in full eighteenth-century costume. "All because I am a Sex Symbol," he said happily. "Look at those legs, baby. Drool at the thought." Shaw patted a muscular thigh with obvious affection. "That's what they want out there in the dark and I got it."

"Keep it, please."

Jim had never seen an actor in full makeup. He was quite awed by the transformation. This was not the man he knew but someone else, a glamorous stranger. As usual, Shaw was conscious of the effect he was making. He gave Jim a conspiratorial grin.

"What sort of picture is it?" asked Jim.

"Shit," said Cy, quietly.

"Popular entertainment," said Shaw. "Which will gross four million domestic. It's a remake of this classic French novel by Dumas *fils*," he added in a rehearsed voice, suitable for instructing interviewers in the commissary.

"Dumas *fils* was the Ronald Shaw of his day, God help him." Cy stood up. "So let's get down to the set. The Bitch Goddess is already there."

Shaw explained to Jim that the Bitch Goddess was his costar, a famous lady whose presence in a film guaranteed success. The combination of Shaw and this lady was considered especially potent.

"She hungover?" asked Shaw as they stepped from the bungalow into the main street of the studio.

"At dawn, her eyes were like two rubies," said Cy, dreamily. "And her breath was reminiscent of a wind in summer over the Jersey Flats."

Shaw grimaced. "We got a love scene?"

"Kind of." Cy handed him two pages. "That's it. Straight from the back of the menu of the Cotton Club. You'll love it."

As they walked, Shaw studied the two pages intently. Jim noticed that all the marvelously dressed people who crowded the studio street stared enviously at Shaw; and Jim took vicarious pride in this attention. Just in front of the soundstage, Shaw handed Cy the script. "I got it," he said.

"You mean you learned it, which isn't exactly getting it."

"Quickest study in the business." Shaw turned to Jim. "I've got this photographic memory. I can see the whole page in my head when I'm acting."

"And that's just about what comes across." Cy was mocking. "Shaw even gives you the typos. Remember that time you said, 'But where is your hubsand'?"

"Knock it off," said Shaw, and all badinage ended as they stepped onto the soundstage, where he was in his proper kingdom. The Bitch Goddess, looking extraordinarily beautiful, lay on an incline board in order not to crush her elaborate costume. When she saw Shaw, she shouted in her celebrated hoarse voice, "Hiya, Butch!"

"You got the new scene?" Shaw was flat.

His costar held up the pages. "It's even worse than the old scene."

"Academy Award time," said Shaw lightly.

"Academy Award? We'll be lucky not to end up in radio when this turkey hits the nabes." She threw the script down.

Then Cy came over. "Ready, folks?" Obediently, they followed him to the center of the set. He then talked to them in a low voice, rather like a boxing referee before a bout. The rules understood, Cy yelled, "Places!" The extras fell into position, some talking in groups of three or four, some ready to walk slowly from group to group when the action started. A buzzer sounded and Cy shouted, "Start moving, children! Let it roll!" There was silence on the soundstage. As the camera approached the female star, she turned, smiling, then, seeing Shaw to her left, she looked surprised.

"Why did you come?" Her voice was clear, the question vital.

"You knew I would." Shaw's voice was resonant and warm. Jim barely recognized it.

"But . . . my husband . . ."

"I've taken care of him. Get your cloak. Quickly! We must leave tonight for Calais."

"Cut!" yelled Cy. The room became noisy again. "Let's take that over again. Shaw, remember to keep your left shoulder down when you walk into range. Darling, try and remember to show surprise when you see him. After all, you think that your husband has had him locked up. OK. We'll take it again."

Jim watched them do this scene for several hours. At the end of the day he was no longer interested in acting.

V

DECEMBER CAME AND JIM found it hard to imagine that it was winter, for the sun continued warm and the trees green. And he was able to play tennis every day. He was beginning to make money, and acquire a reputation as a good teacher. When a magazine photographer came to take pictures of Shaw's house, he also took pictures of Jim. These were published in a fan magazine. As a result, Jim got many offers to give lessons, which he accepted. Offers of another sort he sternly rejected.

Although Shaw approved of his earning money, he disliked it when Jim left the house. One night when Jim did not come home until after dinner, Shaw accused him of being ungrateful and thoughtless. They shouted at one another until Jim went to his room, angry at being treated like a possession. It was even worse later, when Shaw came to his room to say that he was sorry, and to make love, and to tell Jim how great the love was he had to give but how hopeless it all was knowing that such deep feeling could never be returned. Jim could not help but think that perhaps Shaw had less to give than he suspected.

As Jim lay very still in the dark, his arm beneath Shaw's head, he wondered if he should at least speak up and say that he wanted to be free to go wherever he pleased and see people he wanted to see without giving excuses to a lover who was not in love. But Shaw divined his mood.

"I'm sorry I'm so jealous, Jimmy, but I hate to think of your being out with anybody else. I depend a lot on you when I'm tired and want to get away from all these hangers-on. You're different from all the others. You really are. And, God, I'd love to quit this whole racket one of these days. Get out of this town of fakes and go off somewhere in the country and buy a farm maybe. Then Mamma could come live there with us. Of course we'd have to be a little careful with her around, but we could manage. Yes, I'd like that, wouldn't you?"

Jim moved uneasily in the dark. His arm was beginning to go to sleep beneath Shaw's head; he clenched his fist, trying to restore circulation.

"I don't know, Ronnie. I don't know if I'd like to settle down just yet."

"Oh." Shaw's sigh was bitter and stagy. "You really don't give a damn, do you? It's the same old routine: upward and onward. Whores of the world, unite. Because of me, you can now make a living with those tennis lessons, if that's what they are. So I'm nothing to you." Shaw moved over to the other side of the bed and Jim was relieved to feel the blood circulating again in his arm.

"That isn't true, Ronnie. I like you a lot but I haven't had an awful lot of experience with this sort of thing before. I'm still pretty new at it" (he had never told Shaw about Bob) "and I don't think you're being very fair. You can't expect me to give up my whole life when I don't know but what you might find another guy you like more than me, and where'd I be then?"

"What would you do if you did leave me?" Shaw's voice was distant.

"I'd like to start a tennis school maybe. That's what I'm saving for." Jim realized that he had said too much; he had not wanted Shaw to know that he was carefully saving money, three thousand dollars so far.

"You're not really planning to leave?" Shaw was plaintive.

"Not until you want me to," said Jim simply, making up for his blunder.

After breakfast Christmas morning, Shaw telephoned his mother in Baltimore and talked to her for half an hour, regardless of the cost. Then he gave presents in front of the tree. Jim received an expensive Australian tennis racket. Next came dinner at one o'clock, the high point of the day.

Shaw had invited a dozen guests, old friends, men without families who had no place to go at Christmas. Jim knew them all except one, a sandy-haired young man who was talking intensely to Cy. Through the window, Jim caught a glimpse of a palm tree. No, it was not really Christmas, he thought as he said hello to Cy, who looked like a Persian vizier from one of his own pictures. Drunk and merry, he introduced Jim to the sandy-haired man.

"Jim Willard, this is the great Paul Sullivan." They shook hands and Jim wondered why Paul Sullivan was great. Then he excused himself and helped Shaw serve eggnog. Shaw's face was flushed; he was in a gay mood.

"Lovely party, isn't it, Jimmy?"

Jim nodded. "Who is this guy Sullivan? Should I know who he is?" Shaw was usually careful to let Jim know who people were and what they did so that he could treat them accordingly. That was Hollywood procedure. In the hierarchy of money, each man was treated with the deference his salary called for.

"He's a writer who writes books and he came out here to work with Cy on a picture. He's a real highbrow, which means he's a real pain, always bitching about Hollywood. These guys take the industry's money, then they complain. He's typical."

At dinner, Shaw carved the turkey. Champagne was served. The guests were happy. And to Jim's inattentive ear, the conversation sounded brilliant. Even though most of it was about movies: who was being signed for what picture, and why.

Sullivan sat beside Jim. He was a quiet man, with dark eyes and a slightly upturned nose. His mouth was too full and his ears were too large. But he was attractive.

"You're a writer, aren't you?" Jim spoke respectfully, wishing to make a good impression.

Sullivan nodded. "I came out here to work on a picture but . . ." The voice was light and boyish. Deliberately he left the sentence unfinished.

"You don't like working for movies?"

Sullivan glanced at Cy, who was sitting across from him. "No," he said in a low voice, "I don't like it at all. Are you in this business?"

Jim shook his head. "You write books, don't you?"

Sullivan nodded.

"Novels?"

"Novels, poetry. I don't suppose you've read any of them." This was said sadly, not defensively.

"I don't expect so." Jim was truthful. "I don't seem to find time to read."

"Who does in this damned town?"

"I guess they like their work," said Jim uncertainly. "They think about pictures mostly."

"I know." Sullivan ate a stalk of celery and Jim watched him, wondering if he liked him. Most of the people who visited Shaw seemed all alike. They said what they thought about everything, including themselves, and usually they liked themselves rather more than other people did. Sexually they were obvious, unlike Sullivan, who appeared perfectly normal.

"Are you from the East?" asked Jim.

Sullivan nodded. "New Hampshire originally but I live in New York."

Then Sullivan asked Jim many questions and Jim answered most of them truthfully. It was a bit like a cross-examination. Jim had never known anyone to ask so many questions. By the time dessert was served, Jim had told Sullivan most of the facts of his life. As for Sullivan, he was twenty-eight (Jim thought that was old), married once and divorced, an impressive achievement which explained why he was not like most of the sensitive young men who visited Shaw. Obscurely Jim was glad.

Dinner over, the guests gathered in the drawing room. As usual, a group gathered about Shaw. But Sullivan was not one of them. He sat alone in a window seat, his large hands playing idly with a silver matchbox. Jim joined him.

"A beautiful place," said Sullivan.

"You mean this house or . . ."

"The whole thing. It's idyllic. Like going to Heaven before your time. Perfect climate, bright colors, fantastic houses. And beautiful people with suntans, white teeth, empty heads."

"Like me?"

"Yes. No!" Sullivan laughed. Suddenly he was a boy, and

Jim was captured. "Like our host," said Sullivan. "I'm sorry. I shouldn't have said that. You live with him, don't you?"

"Yes."

"Then he must be all right."

"He is," said Jim, realizing that he should say more but not able to.

"You give tennis lessons on the side?"

"That's how I make my living." Jim tried not to sound kept. But it was no use. The thing was plain enough.

"What would you like to do eventually?"

"Set myself up as a teacher. Buy some courts. But that takes money."

"And *otherwise*, do you know what you want?"

"No," said Jim accurately. "I don't know what I want."

"Neither do I." Sullivan smiled, reminding Jim of Bob. Then he rose to go.

"Would you like to play tennis sometime?" Jim was bold. They made a date and Sullivan left. Not until then did Jim realize that Shaw had been watching them.

CHAPTER

5

I

JIM AND SULLIVAN MET every day, unknown to Shaw, who
suspected but did not know for certain what was happening. The lovers would meet at Sullivan's hotel each noon,
the only time during the day when Sullivan was able to leave
the studio lot. Since Jim was usually the first to arrive, he
would go straight to the room and wash up after the morning's tennis. Then he would lie on the bed and wait for
Sullivan, heart beating fast, surprised to find that he was
excited not only by their lovemaking but also by Sullivan as
a person. He was intrigued because Sullivan never mentioned their affair, destroying Jim's theory that all homosexuals talked continually of love, like Shaw. Reticence was
a relief, while it lasted. But eventually words became necessary. Sullivan's contract with the studio was ending. Soon
he would leave California. That meant they needed to

understand one another before plans could be made, *if* plans were to be made.

"How many times have you done this?" Sullivan was abrupt. Jim hesitated, then he told the truth. "Three times. Three different people."

Sullivan nodded. "I thought so."

"What do you mean? Flattery or insult?"

"Just that you haven't followed the usual pattern. I could tell right off. So could Shaw. I expect that's why he wanted you to live with him." This was the first time Sullivan had mentioned Shaw.

"So what's the usual pattern?"

Sullivan lay back on the bed, his eyes on the ceiling. "It starts in school. You're just a little different from the others. Sometimes you're shy and a bit frail; or maybe too precocious, too handsome, an athlete, in love with yourself. Then you start to have erotic dreams about another boy—like yourself—and you get to know him and you try to be his friend and if he's sufficiently ambivalent and you're sufficiently aggressive you'll have a wonderful time experimenting with each other. And so it begins. Then you meet another boy and another, and as you grow older, if you have a dominant nature, you become a hunter. If you're passive, you become a wife. If you're noticeably effeminate, you may join a group of others like yourself and accept being marked and known. There are a dozen types and many different patterns but there is almost always the same beginning, not being like the others."

"I'm pretty ordinary," said Jim, almost believing himself.

"Are you? Perhaps. Anyway you started late and I don't think you're much involved with others. I don't think you could ever love a man. So I hope you find the right woman for yourself." Sullivan stopped. Jim did not answer. He had not told Sullivan about Bob, and yet Sullivan had revealed him to himself as just like the others, varying hardly at all from what must be a familiar pattern. With self-knowledge came alarm. If he was really like the others, then what sort of future could he have? Endless drifting, promiscuity, defeat? No. It was not possible. He was different, Bob was different. After all, hadn't he been able to fool everyone, even those like himself, even Sullivan? Deliberately he banished the unsought revelation to that part of his brain where he disposed of unpleasant memories and then, truth disposed of, he found that he was hurt by something Sullivan had said. Was it true that he was so unfeeling in his relationships? Perhaps with Shaw and Sullivan, but not with Bob. Certainly no one had ever felt as desperate and as lonely as he when Bob had left. Yes, he was perfectly capable of love, at least with someone who could be his brother. And though Sullivan was hardly this longed-for twin, at least he was wiser than Shaw and less demanding and Jim felt easy with him, if not candid, and even affectionate.

"I think you're the unluckiest type." Sullivan rolled over on his stomach and looked at Jim. "You'll attract everybody, yet you won't be able to do anything about it. Not really. Oh, maybe someday you'll find a woman who'll suit you, but not a man. You're not like the rest of us, who want a mirror. It's exciting in a way but it's also sad."

"I don't know what you mean," said Jim, who knew exactly but chose to maintain his secret: a memory of a cabin and a brown river. Someday he would relive all that again and the circle of his life would be completed. Meanwhile he would learn about the world and please himself and scrupulously hide his secret from those who wanted him to love.

. . .

In February Sullivan's option was not renewed. A few days later, coincidentally, Shaw took a new boy. Jim tried to avoid the obligatory scene of parting, but Shaw had waited two months for this moment and so it was played through to the end.

Knowing what was coming, Jim packed his bags that morning and tried to leave the house, but Shaw had insisted that they have a "last supper" together, with Jim in the role of Judas. So Jim remained.

Shaw was silent during most of dinner, crown of thorns resting heavily on his brow. Not until after coffee did he speak. He started in a low voice, more in sorrow than in anger. "I suppose you and Sullivan are going to leave town?"

Jim nodded and Shaw smiled gently. "It's such a shame, Jim. I really was counting on you. I really felt that *this* was the one, the big one that would last. In a funny way, I'm kind of innocent. I thought you were different, and you weren't. Not that I'm blaming you," he said quickly, eager to seem fair. "I know it's tough living with somebody like me, and all the people around us trying to break things up. I know, God knows I know, what the temptations are. Only an awfully strong person could resist, a really strong character—or else someone in love. Which you weren't. Not that that was your fault. I don't blame you. How could I?" Not wanting to be interrupted, Shaw was careful to give both sides as he went along. "After all, love is something which few people are capable of. You were too young. And I should have realized that. You can only love yourself, and now that you've gotten the most out of our relationship, you're ready to move on to this writer, this misfit who's just as incapable of feeling as you. Yes, I've heard a lot of things

about Sullivan," said Shaw darkly. "*You* wouldn't believe
what I've heard, of course. You must find them out for yourself. I'm only telling you this now because I'm still very fond
of you, in spite of what you've done, and to show you that
I'm not bitter. As a matter of fact, I'm happy because I've
found Peter, who's coming to live with me." He paused,
ready for the defense. But there was none. Jim stared at him
politely, wondering when he could decently go.

Disappointed, Shaw tried walking on water. "I'm sure
Peter can return the affection I give. At least I hope so. My
bad luck has *got* to end someday. Oh, I hate to sound as if
I'm accusing you, Jim. I'm not. I know how difficult it
must have been for you. You never really cared for me and
at least you were honest; you never *said* you did. But then
since you never said you *didn't*, I hoped and even believed
sometimes that you did care a little. It's only now that I
have Peter that I can regard what we had together, our
affair, detachedly and with *complete* understanding. I see
that you weren't mature enough and that's probably my
fault for trying to attain the impossible." Jim recognized
this last line from one of Shaw's recent films. Tag ends of
scripts tended to work their way into his conversation.

"I hope," Shaw continued, turning the other cheek,
"that you will realize these things about yourself before you
hurt Sullivan, too. Yes, I admit I've been hurt, terribly hurt
by you, but I don't hold it against you. Which is the one
quality I have that you will never find in anyone else. I
always forgive. Will Sullivan?" Jim tried to appear interested
in this new question, which he knew would soon be
answered. It was. "You see, Paul Sullivan is an unusual
person. There's no doubt about that. They got him here for
snob appeal, or so they thought. He's an *intellectual*, and I
suppose in Greenwich Village the left-wingers think he's
wonderful, though he's never written a real best-seller or

anything anybody has ever read. I certainly haven't. Not that I have much time for reading, but at least I've read all the classics—Walter Scott, Dumas, Margaret Mitchell, all that crowd, and *they* were popular. . . ." He stopped, aware that he was making too much of a case for the popular. "Anyway, it's not important whether he's a good writer or not. The important thing is whether he is capable of feeling, whether he has the maturity to overlook your shortcomings. He was quite cruel to one boy, I'm told. But I'm sure you'll have better luck. I want you to be happy. I really mean it. I do." Shaw's radiant smile almost disguised the hatred in his eyes.

There was a sound in the hall and a dark-haired youth appeared in the doorway.

Shaw rose from the dead. "Come in, Peter, and have some coffee. Jim was just saying good-bye."

II

SULLIVAN WAS THE FIRST person Jim had ever met who found obscure pleasure in his own pain. Obsessed by failure, professional and private, and unable to relieve himself in scenes like Shaw, Paul's only outlet was to write. Yet even in his work he was so studied and inhibited that all he could ever convey was a light bitterness, a casual anger at a world which, all in all, had done well by him. A doting family, until he ceased to be Catholic at sixteen. There was much argument then, but he would not budge. Even the family priest gave him up at last, perfectly bewildered by this unlooked-for apostasy. None suspected that he had forsaken the Church because he was homosexual. For a long time he had tried to exorcise the unnatural spirit, demanding furiously of God that he be freed of this terrible inclination. He prayed continually. But in the end, God failed him, and he turned to Hell. He studied a book on witchcraft, celebrated a Black Mass, tried to sell his soul to the devil in order to be free of lust. But the devil had no use for him either, and so Paul Sullivan abandoned all religion.

For a time Paul was happy. If only in this one act, he had at least demonstrated that he could be free. But his happiness did not last long. At school he fell in love with a young athlete. It was months before he summoned up the nerve to speak to him. During this time he could do nothing more than sit near him in class, watch him play football, and wait. Finally, late one afternoon when everyone else had gone home, they met in front of the school. The boy spoke first. It was easy after that. Though Paul was thin and shy, he had always been accepted as one of the boys. Since he was admired because he was known to read a lot, an athlete would not lose caste by being his friend. So it began. Together they experimented with sex and Paul was as happy as he would ever be again in his life, and perfectly pleased that Heaven and Hell had forsaken him.

But the next year everything changed. The athlete liked girls and they liked him, and so Paul was abandoned and suffered accordingly. He became shyer, more aloof than before. He made no friends. His parents worried about him. His mother was certain that his unhappiness came from the denial of God and Church. He let her believe this, unable to tell her what it was that set him apart from others and made him feel obscurely superior to all the heterosexual world, if only because he had a secret that they could not guess and an insight into life that they did not have. Yet simultaneously he hated himself for needing the body of another man to be complete.

Women were attracted to him, particularly older women, and they were kind to him and, as a result, Paul learned a good deal about women at a time when his contemporaries were learning only about girls' bodies. But this knowledge had its price. Imperceptibly, these amiable companions would begin to presume that conversational intimacy might lead to something else. When that happened, flight was in order.

At seventeen Paul went to Harvard. For the first time in his life he found himself in a tolerant environment. He soon made a number of friends, all of whom were going to write books. Spurred by them, he concentrated on writing. When his father suggested that perhaps he should prepare for the Business School, he reacted so strongly that the subject never came up again.

In college Paul wrote his first novel, about a young man who wanted to be a novelist. (Thomas Wolfe was popular that year.) The novel was rejected by every publisher he sent it to. He also wrote poems; several were published in little magazines. Confident that he was a poet, he left Harvard without a degree, went to New York, broke off all communication with his family, did odd jobs, and wrote a novel about a bitter young man who did odd jobs in New York. The prose was crude, the politics Marxist, the dislike of Catholicism authentic. The book was published and he found himself with the reputation of a person of promise, living in New York with other persons of promise.

One day, in a spirit of rebellion against his nature, Paul married a girl his own age. The marriage was not consummated. He loathed the bodies of women. He liked their faces but not their bodies. As a child he remembered watching his mother undress and being horrified by her sagging body. Since then all women were associated with his mother, not only taboo but unaesthetic. His wife left him and the marriage was annulled.

Paul had many affairs. Some for physical relief, some as

the result of boredom, a few for love or what he thought was love. These all ended badly; he never knew exactly why. Of course the men that he liked were usually simple athletic types, bisexual, who preferred the safety of family life to the edgy pleasures of a homosexual affair, and so he turned to those bars where he could always find a boy who would spend the night with him, in cold blood as it were, through callousness, giving him the pain he had come to expect and secretly need. He lived alone and saw few people. He traveled a good deal and he wrote novels. He put everything into his novels. Yet the result was disappointing. His books were praised but not taken seriously. He made enough money to live but he was not a best-seller. He had an honest contempt for the bad novels that sold well and yet he secretly envied their authors, damned by reviewers but wealthy. Nevertheless, he continued to write. There was nothing else to do, no other life for him but the surrogate one of putting words on paper.

As Paul got older, he deliberately opened himself wide to suffering, and he was not disappointed. He even gained strength. But the bitterness never left him, and at heart he remained the same furious boy who had performed the Black Mass. He was secretly convinced that sooner or later the devil would grant him complete and reciprocated love, whether man or woman made no difference. He would exchange his soul for that.

After a time, Paul became so used to his loveless estate that he had to discover new and more subtle tortures for himself. So he decided to follow in the wake of all those legendary damned souls who had deserted their art for a rich suffering among the orange groves of California. After a long negotiation (it is never easy to sell out) a movie studio agreed to give him the price his agent had demanded and he moved to Hollywood, where he was depressed to find that he really rather enjoyed himself. But fortunately he met Jim and found that he was still vulnerable. Their affair looked to be most promising, with endless possibilities of disaster.

After the break with Shaw, Jim and Sullivan went to New Orleans. Here they stayed in a large hotel in the modern part of the city, while they explored the French Quarter with its narrow dirty streets, low buildings, iron galleries, long shuttered windows, and of course a thousand bars and restaurants, particularly along Bourbon Street, which echoed day and night with jazz and blues music, as everyone prowled: men from ships and men from the country, looking for dark, wiry-haired girls who giggled and looked at them impudently and hinted at "the good time" to come.

In spite of the heat, night in New Orleans was stimulating. So much promise in the air, so much pleasure to be had. One by one like the stations of the Cross, Jim and Sullivan visited the bars, listening to Negro singers, observing the men and the whores. It was a pleasant way to pass time, without guilt or any sense of future.

In the mornings Sullivan would work on a novel (a story of unreciprocated love told with light bitterness) and Jim would go sightseeing. In the afternoons they would go to the YMCA to swim.

In the evenings they would visit queer bars, pretending to be innocent tourists and fooling no one.

A bar called Chenonceaux particularly intrigued them. On the edge of the Quarter, in a quiet street, it occupied all of an old stone building from whose walls most of the plaster had fallen. At one end of the room a small fire burned on a stone hearth, while candles burned and the jukebox played soft popular songs. The result was so soothing that even the wildest patrons tended to behave themselves at the bar, their cries muted, their sibilants hushed, their cruising become demure.

Jim and Sullivan always sat near the fire, where they could watch the men and women come and go, acting out their various rituals of courtship for the benefit of strangers.

As Sullivan watched the menagerie, he would talk in a low voice, saying many things that he would not say in other places, and Jim listened to him, waiting as always to learn something new about himself. But Sullivan spoke only of others.

In March Jim was twenty, and he found himself brooding on the many things he had done and seen since he left Virginia; it was almost as if he had been deliberately courting odd experiences in order to be able to tell of them when he was an old man, sitting in a Virginia store with other old men, none of whom had had so many adventures. Not of course that he would be able to tell everything. At times he wondered if Bob was leading the same sort of life. Was Bob like himself? He hoped not. Yet if they were proper twins, he would have to be the same. It was not easy to sort out. But one day he would know the answer. Now he gave himself up to experience.

Jim's birthday was celebrated at Chenonceaux's by the owner, a fat motherly man who had once been a decorator in New York but was now "reformed." Though he knew only their first names, he suspected that they were wealthy or important or both, but he was far too discreet to ask for information which was not volunteered. Besides, these two young men were much admired by the other patrons, and that was good for business.

"Paul, Jimmy, how're you tonight?" He smiled at Jim, his favorite, and Jim smiled back. He liked the owner despite the motherly ways.

"What'll it be?" They ordered beer and he brought it to them himself. Then he sat down at their table.

"What's the gossip?" asked Paul.

"Well, you'd never guess it, but that tall pale boy, you know the one who used to make such eyes at Jim . . . well, he's gone off with a *Negro* truck driver! It's the funniest thing to see those two together. They're quite wrapped up in each other and I understand the Negro beats him regularly. Really, it's the funniest thing!" They agreed that it was indeed funny, and Jim wanted to know if many Negroes were that way; he had always supposed that they were not.

The fat man rolled his eyes. "Loads of them, literally loads of them! Of course, I expect being a Negro in America is enough to make anyone neurotic. So this added bit, this extra kick, is nothing to be surprised at. Then of course many of them are truly primitive, and primitives don't seem to mind *what* they do if it's fun."

"We should all be like that," said Sullivan.

The fat man frowned; thought of any sort was an effort. "But we have to have *some* conventions, some order, or everyone would be running around wild, committing murder and everything."

"I meant only the sexual taboos, which shouldn't be the business of the law."

"Maybe they shouldn't be but they certainly are! The times I've been picked up by plainclothesmen who made *all* the advances, just awful. Sometimes it costs you a hundred dollars or more to pay off. They're such crooks, especially here."

"Which is all wrong!" Jim could see that Paul was angry. "Why should any of us hide? What we do is natural, if not 'normal,' whatever that is. In any case, what people do together of their own free will is their business and no one else's."

The fat man smiled. "But do you have the nerve to tell the world about yourself?"

Paul sighed and looked at his hands. "No," he said, "I don't."

"So what can we do, if we're all too frightened?"

"Live with dignity, I suppose. And try to learn to love one another, as they say."

"Fair enough," said the fat man. "I have to get back to the bar." He left them.

"Do you really care?" asked Jim. "Do you really care that much about the rest of the world?"

Paul shrugged. "Sometimes, yes. Sometimes I care very much."

They drank their beer and watched the people.

In many ways, the women were the most pathetic. Particularly one old woman who was known as the Major. Gray hair cut like a man's and dressed in a skirted suit with a somber tie, she made a great fuss over the pretty girls, particularly the ones who were shy and clinging.

"There," said Jim, motioning to the Major, "there's somebody honest. You want to be like that?"

"That isn't what I meant. I just want a little simple honesty, and acceptance. Why anyone is anything is a mystery, and not the business of the law."

Jim changed the subject. "How long do you want to stay in New Orleans?"

"Why? Are you bored?"

"No, but I've got to go to work one of these days . . . that tennis deal, I told you about it before."

"Relax. You've got a lot of years to do all that in. Save your money. Have a good time. Wait."

Jim was relieved that neither he nor Sullivan pretended they were going to live together forever. But it did not occur to him how much it hurt Sullivan, who was almost in love, to be so casual. Since they did not understand one another, each was able to sustain an illusion about the other, which was the usual beginning of love, if not truth.

They were joined by a handsome blonde lesbian girl who looked not unlike the Apollo Belvedere, reproduced in plaster. She was much in demand.

"Hiya, boys! Got a drink for your best girl?" They had the drink.

III

THE DAYS PASSED QUICKLY and Jim enjoyed living without purpose. He was happy to get up in the morning; he was happy to go to bed at night with the thought of a new day to look forward to. He knew his life was aimless, and he could not have been more content.

Suddenly the war in Europe occupied even the attention of the people in Chenonceaux's bar. They discussed whether or not Britain would be invaded, and it seemed that everyone had some sentimental reminiscence about Stratford or Marble Arch or Guardsmen in Knightsbridge. Rather self-consciously, people became absorbed by the bit of history through which their century was passing.

By the end of May, New Orleans had begun to bore them. Jim spoke of going to New York to work, while Paul thought they should go to South America; but he was not insistent; he merely indicated that he would like to continue with Jim for a while longer. Then, unexpectedly, their course was set for them.

One night at the Chenonceaux, while talking to the

owner, Jim saw a woman enter the bar, quite alone. She was dark, exotic, well-dressed, impossible to classify. Diffidently she ordered a drink. She attracted the owner's attention. "Oh, dear!" He looked distraught. "This one's come to the wrong bar. I can tell a mile off!" He got to his feet. "We'll lose our reputation, if civilians start coming here." He crossed to the bar, scowling. Then Sullivan recognized the woman at the same time she recognized him.

"Paul!" she exclaimed and she took her drink from the bar and joined them. Whoever she was, Paul was delighted to see her. When he introduced her to Jim, she gave him a genuine smile, showing interest but not curiosity, for which he was grateful.

Jim watched her face as she talked, thin eyebrows arched naturally, hazel eyes, dark hair. Slim with an unobtrusive figure, she moved like a dancer.

She spoke of Amelia, Sullivan's ex-wife. "Where is she now?" asked Paul.

"Still in New York, I think." Maria's accent was all her own, delicate and evocative.

"Do you think she'll get married again?"

"I doubt it. But who knows? She works for a magazine. I saw her just a week ago. She's now developed a large . . . *world*-consciousness. She's interested in nothing so small as the marriage of two human beings. She thinks only of the masses and the spirit of history. At the moment she is violently against the Russians because they are pro-Hitler. Ten months ago she was a Stalinist. I'm afraid she's abandoned all thought of a private life. She is entirely public, and most formidable."

Jim listened with interest. Sullivan seldom mentioned his brief career as a married man. "Poor Amelia," said Sullivan finally. "She hasn't had a very happy time of it. Is she making money?"

Maria nodded. "I should think so. In that world she's quite well thought of."

"What have *you* been doing, Maria?"

She laughed. "Nothing, as always. But it keeps me busy. I was in France until the autumn. Then the war started and I came back to New York, where I was very proper."

"Do you ever hear from Verlaine?"

She frowned slightly and made sketches on the table with her long fingers. "He's in the Army, I understand. No, I haven't heard anything from him. I haven't seen him in years."

"Are you painting still?"

"No," she said. "How was Hollywood?"

Paul grinned. "It was perfect, until they asked me to write something for them and then of course I had to go."

Maria laughed. "Still Don Quixote?"

"I'm afraid so." Sullivan was obviously delighted at being thought impractical yet pure of heart.

They were silent. Jim studied the smooth, well-cared-for face of Maria Verlaine, aware that the more he looked at her the more beautiful she became. Finally Sullivan asked her what she was doing in New Orleans.

"I'm en route."

"To any place, or just in general?"

"In general. But most immediately to Yucatán."

"What a curious place."

"I have a reason. My father died last winter and left me a plantation where they grow whatever it is you make rope out of. Now I have an offer to sell the place. They need me there."

"Is it civilized?"

"No, but it's near Mérida, which is a proper city."

Sullivan turned to Jim and saw that he was looking at

Maria Verlaine. He frowned, but neither noticed. "And you," Maria asked, "are you en route?"

Sullivan shrugged. "No destination that I know of. Jim and I just drift."

"I see." And it seemed that she did. Then: "Why don't you drift with me? They say Mérida's fascinating, full of ruins, and if sightseeing gets dull, you can always fly up to Mexico City. Oh, do say you'll come! It will save my life." And so it was decided that they would travel together.

In their hotel room Jim asked Sullivan about Maria. Sullivan was unusually communicative. "She was married to a Frenchman, a bit of a gigolo. They were divorced. She's had a number of affairs, usually with artists, always doomed. Of course she's the Isolde sort. Also, she's attracted to difficult men, particularly homosexuals, and they usually find her attractive, too. Don't you? I do. I even went to bed with her years ago."

Jim wondered if this was true. "She seems very nice," he said cautiously.

"You'll like her. That's a promise." They got into bed. Sullivan was enormously pleased with himself. He had now endangered his affair with Jim. He had deliberately brought him into contact with the one woman who might appeal to him. There was now an excellent chance that he would lose Jim, and the thought gave him a profound and bitter pleasure. He would suffer. He would know pain. With infinite care and patience, he set about destroying his own happiness.

CHAPTER

6

I

YUCATÁN IS A FLAT land of low scrub jungle and sisal fields. The capital city of Mérida is close to the Gulf of Mexico. Sisal plantations surround the city and, from the air, travelers can see the white pyramids of Chichén Itzá and Uxmal, the ancient Mayan cities. So much for the guidebook.

As they drove from the airport to a hotel in the center of town, the driver pointed out the cathedral, a baroque church with many cracks in its stucco walls, overlooking a great plaza filled with shade trees. Here the natives sat on stone benches, small and brown with faces more Indian than Spanish. Small ragged boys scurried about the plaza, shining shoes and playing games with tops.

Once a private house, the hotel was a large square pink building whose interior smelled like the inside of an ancient cigar box, musty and stale. A tall bandit with a thick mus-

tache welcomed them. He was the manager and had known
Maria Verlaine's father. He treated them like royalty as he
showed them their rooms.

Jim and Sullivan were given a three-room suite decorated
in French Provincial bordello, with a smoky glass chande-
lier, a tile floor, and two great beds shrouded in mosquito
netting. "You will like, yes?" Yes, they would like. And they
did. Jim even got used to sleeping in the middle of the day.
As for Maria, she was at last removed from a world that had
come to bore her; also, she enjoyed being with Jim, aware
that a flirtation was now inevitable. He in turn was attracted
to her but he was not sure in what way. The game was new
to him. He had to learn the rules as he went along. Meanwhile, the opening moves had been made.

Sullivan knew with a curious prescience exactly what
would happen. He was like God. He had arranged a set of
circumstances, and now all that he needed to do was to wait
for the expected climax.

After the first week of sightseeing, they did not go about
much in the town. Men would come in the morning to talk
business with Maria. Sullivan would read and Jim would go
swimming at the mineral baths. Nothing more strenuous
was possible, the heat was too enervating.

Then Sullivan began to drink heavily. Jim was shocked.
Sullivan had seldom drunk before. Now he drank steadily
through the day so that by dinnertime he was ready for bed.
Politely, if shakily, he would excuse himself, insisting that
Jim stay with Maria and keep her company.

One evening after Sullivan had gone to bed, Jim and
Maria sat down together in the patio. A crescent moon
shone white and clear in the black night, and a breeze
rustled the fronds of the palm trees.

"I know how difficult it is." Maria guessed his mood.
"Paul's a strange man, so bitter about everything. Every-

one. When you praise another writer, it hurts him, even if you're praising Shakespeare. If you say you like people with dark hair, he'll be hurt because his hair isn't dark. And now he has turned completely away from people. I don't know why. In the old days he was different. He was more . . . alive. He felt that he had been given great insight, greater than anyone else's, and he regarded it as a sacred gift, which it is, though perhaps the gift was never so great as he thought."

"But he's very good, isn't he?" Jim wanted to know.

"Yes," said Maria quickly, "he's very good. But not good enough. Not as good as he wanted to be. I think that hurts him."

"Is it so important, being a great writer?"

She smiled. "It's important to those who think it's important, who've given up everything to be great."

"Has Paul given up so much?"

"Who can tell? Is he capable of love?"

The question was direct, and Jim blushed. "I . . . I don't know. I think so." But Jim was not at all certain that he knew what love was. He assumed that it must be something like what he felt for Bob, an emotion which, as he grew older, became even stronger, as though absence in some way preserved it pure. Also what he felt had the virtue of being unstated, a secret all his own. He smiled, thinking of this, and Maria said, "What amuses you?"

"I was just thinking how far I am from Virginia, from the town I was raised in. I was thinking how different my life is from all the rest of them back there."

She misunderstood. "Do you mind it very much, being different?"

It was the first time she had made direct reference to the affair with Sullivan, and he hated her for mentioning it, furious at being marked. "I'm not as different as all that."

"I'm sorry." Aware of her mistake, she touched his arm. "I was clumsy."

Jim forgave her, but not completely. Obscurely, he wanted to hurt her, to throw her on a bed and take her violently against her will, to convince himself and her and everyone that he was not like the others. A pulse beat in his throat. He was afraid, even as they talked lightly of other matters.

Sullivan was reading when Jim came upstairs. He looked a ghostly figure beneath the mosquito netting. "Have a nice time?"

"What do you mean by that?" Jim was ready for battle.

"With Maria, you know what I mean. She's attractive, isn't she?"

"Sure. Sure." Jim let his clothes drop to the floor; the night was hot; he was suddenly weary.

"Wait till you know her better. She's a marvelous lover."

"Shut up."

"Just wait. That's all. Just wait." He grinned drunkenly. Jim cursed him. Then he turned out the lights and got into his own bed. It was several hours before he could sleep.

II

MARIA VERLAINE WAS A curious woman, subtle, not easily apprehended. At forty she seemed a girl, slender, expectant, dreamy, her whole life devoted to that desire and pursuit of the whole which obsesses the romantic and confounds the rest. She moved from affair to affair, drawn to the sensitive, the delicate, the impossible. Her imagination could transform the most ordinary of men into dream-lovers, if the occasion were right and his response sufficient. But in time imagination flagged. Reality intruded, and the affair would end, usually in flight. Yet she continued like some gallant warrior committed to a losing cause; after all, her favorite legend was that of Don Quixote and the impossible quest. Believing this, she had made it her life. But as time passed, she found herself drifting more and more toward men younger than herself, to youths whose delicacy was almost feminine. Adolescents could often give gentleness for gentleness, heightened awareness for heightened awareness, and of course they too believed in love. But she usually stopped short of homosexuals. She had lived too long in Europe. Too many of her contemporaries had been captured by the league of dressmakers and decorators, and she had vowed that she would not be trapped by them, though they amused her, made her laugh, treated her as a confidante. Yet out of kindness, not malice, they tried to unsex her and make her one of them. Fortunately, she had a genius for flight. She knew when to leave without inflicting pain. So they allowed her a temporary visa in their world, and she enjoyed being a tourist.

Now she was attracted to Jim. He was exotic to her. Never before had she been attracted to an ordinary man, much less a boy. Aesthetically he pleased her. She had always been drawn to the Nordic gods. Blue eyes, blond hair, pale skin intrigued her. Did they feel anything at all, these silvery northerners? Were they quite human? But more to the point, he touched her. He was so completely locked in himself, inarticulate, without means of communication, with nothing to offer but his body, which he used almost as a sacrifice to propitiate some dangerous god. She wanted him. If there was some silver Nordic mystery, she wanted to partake of it. She hesitated only because of Paul. At a signal from him she would withdraw. But the signal never came, and she took this to mean complaisance.

One afternoon she drove with Jim in a horse-drawn carriage to a pool where they often swam. Sullivan had stayed at the hotel.

"How long do you think it'll be before your business is done?" asked Jim.

"I don't know. I really don't know. They're so slow here. In a few weeks, perhaps. You must be terribly bored."

"No, I'm not bored. Not yet, anyway. I even like hot weather. But I want to go to New York before the fall."

"And start playing tennis again?"

"Yes, I like to work."

"Will you live in New York with Paul?" The question was asked.

Jim paused. "Maybe. But I'm on my own." The question was answered.

"What did you do in Hollywood?"

"Taught tennis. Not much."

"Hollywood must be interesting. I've never been there for very long. Did you know . . ." She mentioned names and he answered "yes" or "no." Then, subtly, she asked names of homosexual figures; he answered "yes" to many of them. They talked, finally, of Shaw.

"I met him once in New York. I thought he was a vain little man."

"He's not so bad when you know him." Jim was loyal. "He isn't very happy, God knows why. He has everything."

"Except what he wants."

"I don't think he knows what he wants, like the rest of us."

Maria was amused: she had underrated Jim. "I expect you're right. Not many people know. And even when they do, it's not easy finding it."

"I think I'd like money," said Jim. "Enough to live any-way."

"Is that all?"

"Well, there's one other thing."

"And that?"

"Is my secret." He laughed.

The summer passed. Maria's business was done but they did not leave. Sullivan drank. Jim swam with Maria and looked at ruins. The heat was almost palpable. To cross a street left one wet with perspiration. But they remained, and no one spoke of leaving, not even Jim.

All three were waiting.

One day they visited the ruins of Chichén Itzá and stayed overnight in the adjacent inn, where they were picked up by a couple from Seattle named Johnson. The Johnsons were young, lively, and innocent. Mrs. Johnson ("I read every-thing") was thrilled to meet Sullivan. Actually, she had read only one of his books and had forgotten what it was about. Even so, she was excited at meeting a genuine author.

That night, after dinner, they sat outside among the palm trees and Mrs. Johnson did most of the talking. They were all pleasantly drowsy. Maria sat with her hands folded in her lap, looking at the ruins in the distance: pyramids and square ornate buildings monstrous by starlight. Jim tried to hide his yawns. He wanted to go to bed. Sullivan drank tequila and Mrs. Johnson's praise.

"I really do envy you writers. You have such a good time going around from place to place. You know, I used to think I'd be a writer. You know, somebody like Fannie Hurst. But I guess I had more important things to do." She looked fondly at her husband.

"Yes," said Sullivan. "I'm sure you did."

"Are you married, Mr. Sullivan? If you'll excuse me being personal."

"I'm divorced."

"Oh, now that's a pity. This may surprise you, but I didn't really *live* until George and I were married. But I expect you'll be getting married again, Mr. Sullivan. I mean a distinguished man like yourself and still young . . ."

"I don't think so."

"That's what they all say!" Mrs. Johnson chattered gaily about marriage and its heady pleasures.

Jim always felt oddly superior when he was with normal people who assumed that everybody shared their tastes. If they only knew, he thought, smiling to himself in the dark. He glanced at Maria and saw that she was sitting still as the statue they had seen that day among the ruins, a goddess with a skull mask. Paul had laughed when he saw the stone figure; he found it significant that the only goddess in the Mayan hierarchy was Death.

"Are you a writer, too, Mrs. Verlaine?" The Johnsons had decided that these three people were a bit unusual, traveling together, but that they were probably *all right*. If they weren't all right, then it was even more interesting.

"No," said Maria, "I am nothing."

"Oh." Mrs. Johnson turned to Jim, but then decided not to question him; he looked too young to have done anything worth talking about.

"Don't you find the Indians here absolutely charming, Mr. Sullivan?"

"In what way?"

"Well, they're so basic and yet . . . inscrutable. I think they're probably quite happy even if they are poor. Certainly it'd be a mistake to educate them. They'd just be miserable, that's all." She talked awhile about Indians. Then, inevitably, they spoke of the movies.

Mrs. Johnson saw almost as many movies as she read books. She was happiest when she was seeing a movie made from a book that she had read. She always remembered every character and she disliked unfaithful representations. "Of course my favorite actor is Ronald Shaw. He's so *force-ful*. I happened to be reading in a movie magazine—I see them at the hairdresser, they always seem to have them— and I read where he was going to marry that Spanish actress Carlotta Repollo, who is years older than he is. Such a pity, don't you think?"

Sullivan glanced at Jim, who blushed. Maria was also amused. Three people in disguise were performing a play for an audience that could never know or appreciate the quality of the performance.

"I should like to see the ruins," said Maria suddenly.

"By starlight?" Sullivan was mocking. "Well, why not? You take her, Jim."

"Well . . ." He looked at Maria.

"I think we should all go," she said.

"No. You two go. You're the romantic ones."

The Johnsons looked at the trio, aware of undertones. Then Maria left the table and Jim followed her. They walked out of the small square of electric light and into the darkness. The starlight made no shadows in the cool night. Like disembodied spirits, they walked down an avenue of cropped grass and then, at the same instant, without words, they sat down side by side on the shattered stone remains of a forgotten god.

Jim looked up at the stars, brilliant and white in the black sky. He breathed deeply. There was the scent of sage in the air as well as the dry odor of sunburned stone.

He turned to Maria and saw that she was waiting. He was surprised that he was not afraid.

"One feels dead here." Her voice was distant and remote among the ruins.

"Dead?"

"In a peaceful way. All things finished, inevitable, like one of these stones: there is to be nothing else."

"*If* death is like that."

"It must be."

They did not speak for a long while. At last Maria spoke. "We've been playacting."

"Yes."

"And dishonest."

"With Paul?"

"With Paul. Ourselves." She sighed. "I wish I knew more about people. I wish I could understand why things are as they are."

"Nobody knows." Jim was amazed to find himself playing at wisdom. "I don't know why I do what I do or even who I am."

"I don't know who you are either." They looked at one another, faces white and indistinct.

"Myself. That's all. Limited."

"Limited? Not really. Actually you're everything, man, woman, and child. You can be whatever you choose."

"What am I now?"

"Until a few moments ago a child."

"What am I now?"

"I don't know."

He began to tremble; he began to hope. Perhaps it could happen.

"Are you afraid?"

"No. Not afraid." Nor was he at that moment.

"Could you kiss me?"

"I could kiss you," he said, and he did. He kissed the Death Goddess.

. . .

Everything was different afterward; different and yet the
same, for nothing finally happened. Jim failed. He could
not perform the act. He was inadequate. Yet in its way, his
relationship with Maria was a love affair. They were with
each other as much as possible. They were confidants. Yet
when it came to physical contact, except for that first kiss,
Jim could not bear the softness and smoothness of a
woman. Maria was baffled. Because he was both masculine
and drawn to her, she found his failure all the more mysterious. There seemed nothing to be done except to continue
as lovers who never touched. Sullivan, however, accepted
the surface affair for an actual one, and the agony it gave
him was exquisite.

November came and still they did not move from Mérida.

Jim and Maria were together most of the time. Sullivan
refused to join them during the day. He had begun to drink
after breakfast; by early evening he was often vivacious and
amusing but by the end of dinner he was inevitably heavy
and bitter. Their lives stopped until December, when the
United States went to war with Japan, and they were once
more part of the world. Sullivan stopped drinking. Plans
were made as they sat in the patio after dinner. Both Sullivan and Jim were excited, brought to life. Maria was sad. "I
don't like to think about it," she said. "All my life there has
been a war, just begun, just finished. There seems to be no
escape."

Sullivan paused in a nervous turn about the patio. "We'll
have to go back," he said to Jim.

Jim nodded, caught up in the drama of new things. "I
want to enlist before I'm drafted," he said, pleased at the
words if not the thought.

"It's so senseless." Maria was vehement. "If I were a man I'd run away, hide, desert, turn traitor."

Sullivan smiled. "Five years ago I would have done just that."

"Why not now?"

"Because this is . . . something to do."

She turned to Jim. "Do you feel the same?"

"It solves a lot of things."

"Perhaps." She seemed unconvinced.

"We should go back as soon as possible," said Sullivan.

"What will you do?" asked Maria.

"Be a soldier. Or a correspondent. Whatever I can get."

"It looks," said Maria, "as if our Mexican vacation is at an end. I've enjoyed it."

"So have I." Jim looked at her and felt a sudden warmth; threat of war and parting drew him closer to her.

"And so have I." Sullivan's voice mocked them. "I've enjoyed every minute of it. We've made an interesting trio, haven't we?"

"Have we?" Maria was bleak.

It was decided that they return to the States by way of Guatemala City.

They rode comfortably above clouds, mountains, dark green jungle. It was pleasant to sail over the hot steaming land as though they were no longer earth creatures but something more than human, elemental, with no difficulties that could not be overcome by rigid silver wings.

Jim had bright visions of himself in the Air Corps, flying across continents and oceans, able to move rapidly over the earth and leave no scar. He longed for flight.

Guatemala City was a relief after Yucatán. The city was cool with streets which looked as if they had been recently scrubbed. The people were cheerful, the air good. And wherever one looked, volcanoes loomed, sharp, veined blue with shadow, topped by rain clouds.

At the hotel, Sullivan sent cables to various newspaper friends who might help him to get an assignment as war correspondent. Then, communication with the real world established, Jim and Sullivan went to their room.

"It's almost over." Sullivan stood at the window, looking at mountains. Jim unpacked.

"The trip?"

"The trip, of course."

"Yes," said Jim, who knew what he meant. "I guess we'll split up when we get to New York."

Sullivan smiled. "I doubt if the Army would send us to war together."

"Everything ends. I wonder why."

"Don't you know?" Sullivan was scornful. "Don't you know?"

"Do you?"

"Certainly. When you fall in love with someone else, that automatically ends the original affair, doesn't it?"

"You mean Maria?"

"Yes, I mean Maria."

"It's . . . a very complicated business, Paul. It's not what it seems to be." But Jim failed to tell the whole truth; it was too humiliating.

Fortunately Sullivan was not interested in facts; his intuition was quite enough; whatever the details were, the result was bound to be the same. "Anyway, I knew all along that this would happen. I let it happen."

"Why?"

But Sullivan could never admit to anyone why he was driven to behave as he did. "Because," he said, and he knew he was not convincing, "I thought it would be the best

thing that could happen to you. She's a wonderful woman.
She can get you out of this world."

"Why should I get out?" For the first time Jim admitted
what he was.

"Because you're never going to fit into this sort of relationship, and so the sooner you find your way to something
else the better it'll be for you."

"Maybe." Jim looked at Paul. The dark circles had gone
from beneath his eyes. He was still attractive to Jim, even
now, when everything was over. They spoke kindly to one
another. Yet finally, each was so perfectly dishonest that
neither was able to feel the slightest regret at what was
ending.

On the last night they dined in a restaurant particularly
recommended for those who wanted native food without
diarrhea. Walls bright with primitive scenes of volcanoes,
conquistadores, flowers, lakes. Rooms loud with the noise
of a small marimba band. Tourist couples danced.

All during dinner Jim felt reckless and glad, like a child let
out of school.

They drank Chilean wine and even Maria was gay. But
toward the end of dinner, when the music grew sad and
sentimental and they had all drunk too much white wine,
they became sad and sentimental, too. But it was the sort of
sadness that is closely related to happiness. Each was now
secure in his own failure. Doubt was gone. Boundaries had
been drawn and accepted.

"It's too sad," said Maria as the band rattled "La Paloma."
"We've lived such a long time together. And played so many
games."

"True." Sullivan was moody. "But it's also a relief to have
things end."

"Some things." Maria twirled her wineglass in her hands. "I think love is always a tragic thing, for everyone, always."

"But that's what makes life interesting. How can we value anything until it's gone?"

"No light without dark?"

"Yes. And no pain without pleasure."

"What a curious way to put it." She looked at him, almost aware of his secret.

"Even so," he said quickly, "there are other things in life than being in love. Look at Jim. He's never in love, are you?"

"Of course I am. With what I want." Jim thought of Bob.

Maria was puzzled. "What do you want?"

Sullivan answered for him. "What he cannot have, like the rest of us." He turned to Maria. "Have *you* ever found what you wanted?"

"For a time, certainly."

"But not for long."

"No, not for long. I've failed, like everyone else."

"Why?"

"I suppose I may want more than any man cares to give. And sometimes I give more than any man wants to take."

"Shaw was like that," said Jim suddenly. "I mean he *thought* he was that way."

"Shaw was an idiot," said Sullivan.

"We all are," said Maria sadly, "at the end."

They were silent. The marimba clattered in the room. They drank more wine. At last Sullivan got up and went to the men's room. For the first time since they had come to Guatemala, Jim was alone with Maria. She turned to him. "I'm leaving tomorrow."

"You're not coming with us?"

"No. I'm not strong enough. You know, sometimes I

believe that there *is* a God, a vindictive, self-righteous God who punishes happiness. I was happy with you when I thought . . ." She could not finish. "Anyway, it will be years before you can love a woman. I haven't the time to wait."

"But you know how I feel about you."

"Yes," she said, and there was no more emotion in her voice. "I know how you feel." She stood up. "I'm going back to the hotel."

He stood up too. "Will I see you before you go?"

"No."

"In New York?"

"Perhaps."

"I'll be able to see you then. I'll want to see you. I don't want to lose you, too."

"When I'm happier, we'll see each other. Good night, Jim."

"Good night, Maria." She left the restaurant quickly, the black lace of her dress rustling about her legs.

Sullivan came back. "Where's Maria?"

"She's gone to the hotel. She was tired."

"Oh? Well, let's have another drink." They drank.

Though sad, Jim was relieved to have a temporary end to emotion. He had been exhausted by these two people, taken out of his depth. Now he looked forward to freedom. Released by the fact of war, he would soon be resolved by action. He could not wait for his own life to begin.

CHAPTER

7

I

JIM AND SULLIVAN ARRIVED in New York in mid-December. Almost immediately Sullivan obtained a job with a news syndicate, while Jim enlisted in the Army. Neither saw Maria Verlaine; she had disappeared.

Jim went first to a reception center in Maryland, where he was put to work tending fires while the Army decided what to do with him. Bad weather and petty tyranny kept him so angry that he had no time for self-pity, as he moved stolidly through the black days, acknowledging the existence of no one else.

Waking up late one afternoon, after an all-night vigil at the coal furnaces, Jim wandered into the recreation room of the company barracks. A dozen new soldiers watched the afternoon pool game, played by two members of the permanent company. Lonely, Jim decided to break his long silence. He turned to the soldier next to him, a man of forty, hopelessly civilian, with a small mustache and sad eyes.

"How long you been here?" asked Jim.

The man looked at him gratefully, a little surprised. "Why, almost a month." The voice was educated, unlike the guttural barks of so many of the new soldiers, recruited from slums and deep country. "And you?"

"Two weeks. I enlisted in New York. Where are you from?"

"Ann Arbor, Michigan. I was with the university."

Jim was impressed. "A teacher?"

The man nodded. "Professor of history, associate professor."

"Then what're you doing here? I thought people like you got to be majors."

The professor laughed nervously. "So did I. But I was wrong. In the age of Demos, only yokels like our first sergeant rise to the top."

"Did you enlist?"

"Yes. I'm married, have two children, but I enlisted."

"Why?"

"I had some strange idea that I'd be useful."

For the first time since Jim had enlisted he was able to feel sorry for someone else. He was pleased at this manifestation of good character. "Rough deal," he said. "What do you think they're going to do with you?"

"Classify me as a clerk. That seems to be my fate."

"Won't you get to be an officer?"

"Perhaps. I have friends in Washington. But I seem to've lost all faith in this business. Of course things were even worse in the Army of the Potomac. The Civil War," he added apologetically.

"Worse in combat now, too." They had all heard horror

stories about the Philippines, where American troops had been badly defeated.

"Perhaps," said the professor, "but I find it hard to believe. This seems like hell, in a way, or a nightmare with no way out of it. We are governed by madmen."

Two large, red-faced country boys approached. They were clumsy and good-humored. "Hey there, Professor, you look like you shot your wad. They gettin' you down?"

"Hello, boys. No, they haven't got me down just yet. I'm simply converting from peace to war at my own slow pace."

One of the boys made a joke about the word *peace*, and the professor laughed as loudly as they did, eager to be their butt. Jim was sad to see him play the buffoon. It was important to remain oneself. Even though he could not acknowledge what he was, he refused to pretend that he was just like everyone else. It hurt him now to see another man sacrifice his pride, particularly when it was not necessary.

The professor kept the red-faced boys laughing by telling them funny stories about his trials on twenty-four-hour KP. They occasionally glanced at Jim to see if he was laughing. But he did not respond and they disapproved. Fortunately, he was larger than they.

The first sergeant, a short man of fifty, came into the room and there was silence except for the click of billiard balls. "I want two men," he said. "I want two volunteers to clean out the goddamn latrine. Some son of a bitch fouled it up and I want two men." Suddenly he swooped down on Jim and the professor. "You two," he said.

"Certainly, Sergeant," said the professor, jumping to his feet. "Always happy to volunteer!"

It took them two hours to clean the latrine, during which time Jim learned a good deal about American history and the tyranny of democratic armies.

II

IN FEBRUARY JIM WAS transferred to Georgia. For the next three months he was busy with his basic training. The physical side of Army life appealed to him; he enjoyed being active, although the minor humiliations continued to annoy him.

In May he was sent to the Air Corps as a general duty man (the usual classification for the unskilled), and shipped out to an air base in Colorado, where he was assigned to the headquarters of a wing which in turn was part of a command which in turn was part of the Second Air Force, devoted largely to training pilots and bombardiers. Of the two hundred men in his unit, most were headquarters personnel. Older than the average soldier, those of noncommissioned rank usually lived off the post with their wives in Colorado Springs.

Jim and his fellow infantrymen were received by the first sergeant, a tall emaciated man who had once been a salesman of household appliances.

"You're in the Air Corps now." He tried to sound ominous. "You may have heard stories that we aren't as tough as some branches, but that's just a crock. You hear me? You hear what I say? We got discipline here, a lot of it. Because this is a pretty important headquarters and don't ever forget it. We got a tough general. So you keep on the line and do your job and you'll be OK."

But the Air Corps was by no means as tough as the infantry. Discipline was spasmodic. The clerks were just like clerks anywhere and Jim was contemptuous of them. Though the wooden tar-papered barracks were gloomy and the food was bad, the life was not unpleasant. For the first months he and the other infantrymen did not associate with the Air Corps clerks; they kept their identity proudly, but inevitably they were absorbed.

One day was very like another. In the early morning a record of reveille was played over the loudspeaker. As the men yawned and swore, the first sergeant charged through the barracks, bellowing at those still asleep. Then they ran through the icy air to the latrine twenty yards away; then came breakfast in the mess hall. Jim downed the greasy food perfunctorily, unaware of what he was eating. Afterward the first sergeant would have a number of jobs for the general-duty men to do. The work was often hard—building barracks, loading garbage trucks, repairing runways. Hard work but not much of it. Jim often had whole days to himself when he would go down to the long runways and watch the B-17s and the B-24s take off and land. The bomber crews were obviously fascinated by what they were doing, unlike the rest of the men, who were listlessly engaged in pointless tasks. Jim was particularly struck by one of the pilots, a roaring boy with blond hair who was particularly popular with the ground crews. He sang popular songs in a loud toneless voice, indulged in horseplay, and generally gave pleasure. Once Jim found himself face to face with him. Jim saluted, but the pilot only grinned and clapped him on the shoulder and said, "Hi!" One boy to another. Jim was dazzled. And that was all. Rank separated them. It was sad.

Jim made no friends. He avoided the nightly bull sessions in the barracks. Instead he saw movies and read books, among them a novel by Sullivan, which seemed to him to be the work of a perfect stranger; no doubt it was. Occasionally he visited Colorado Springs, where he was very much aware of those alert-looking soldiers, forever searching for a response. But Jim ignored them; he had no interest in sex.

Eventually Jim was reclassified. One of the personnel officers, noting that he had been a tennis instructor, put him in
Special Services as a physical-training coach. His life
improved. He got along well with Captain Banks, the
Special Services officer, a football player who had been a
pilot, grounded for reasons of health. Captain Banks moved
dreamily about his office, signing necessary papers, unaware
of what he was doing. Like so many base officers, he had
abdicated all authority to his sergeant.

Sergeant Kervinski was a slim dark man who wore a large
diamond ring on his little finger and talked quickly, blushing often. His delight when Jim was added to the section
was plain even to an innocent eye. Trouble ahead, thought
Jim.

The Special Services detachment consisted of those who
ran the post theater and library, staged plays and radio pro-
grams, edited a newspaper. Along with these mercurial types
there were a half-dozen quiet youths who were physical-
training instructors. But since all efforts at group discipline
were invariably sabotaged by the clerks, Jim had a very easy
time of it. Hardly anyone reported for calisthenics, and the
instructors had the gymnasium to themselves, which suited
them well since they were all dedicated bodybuilders.

Agreeable though the life was, Jim longed to be sent
overseas, even though he knew that in modern armies there
is seldom much action except for line troops and combat
pilots. Nevertheless, he was excited by the thought of
danger. He wanted release. A few of the general-duty men
longed for the same thing. They too hated routine and
inactivity, but they were not in the majority. Each headquarters clerk had at least one officer friend pledged to keep
him from being sent overseas or, if sent, shipped to a rea-
sonably safe place like England. The clerks were not heroes
and they were honest about it. Only Sergeant Kervinski was

different. It was his dream to be sent to a languorous island of white beaches and no women. When Jim asked to be put on the first overseas shipment list, Kervinski told him of this paradise, adding, "I know what you mean, honestly I do, and I'll put you on the list. Perhaps we'll ship out together, to the South Seas. Come on, let's go to supper."

They stood in line together to collect the usual heavy food. Then they sat down at one of the long wooden mess tables. A calendar with a picture of a heavy-breasted woman hung just above Kervinski's head. He glanced at it with distaste. Then he turned to Jim and made an exploratory move. "Some woman!"

"Some woman," Jim repeated flatly.

"I guess you never had the time to get yourself a woman, a wife," said Kervinski brightly. "I mean with your traveling around so much." He knew something of Jim's story.

"No, I never had time." The approach was made even more depressing by the sergeant's unattractiveness.

"Well, they say there's nothing like a wife. But not for me. After all, it's a lot cheaper to buy milk than keep a cow! Isn't it?"

Jim grunted.

"What was Hollywood really like?" Kervinski looked at him eagerly.

"Just like anyplace else." Jim had once shown some of the clerks the movie magazine with his picture in it. They had been sufficiently impressed to dislike him afterward; he had learned his lesson, and now never mentioned the past.

"I understand," said Kervinski, blushing, "that you knew Ronald Shaw and a lot of other stars. What was *he* like?"

The entire underworld knew about Shaw. "I didn't know him well." Jim was evasive. "I just played tennis with him a few times."

"Well, I hear a lot of strange stories about him but I don't
see how they could be true."

"Oh? What sort of stories?" Jim was malicious.

The sergeant turned scarlet. "Oh . . . just stories. The
kind you always hear about Hollywood people. I don't see
how they could be true."

"People always talk."

"By the way," said Kervinski, examining a piece of green,
watery cabbage, "I understand that ratings will be open this
month."

"That so?"

"I've recommended you to the captain for a PFC stripe."
The sergeant put the cabbage in his mouth.

"Thanks a lot," said Jim, fearing the worst.

Kervinski chewed thoughtfully. "We should have dinner
some evening, in town. I know a wonderful restaurant out
near the Broadmoor. We bachelors should stick together,"
he added with a little laugh.

"That would be fine," said Jim, hoping that when he
eventually said no that Kervinski would not be too upset.

"Then," said Kervinski, "there are some girls I know.
They're very nice and I'm sure you'd like them. Do you
know any girls in town yet?"

Jim shook his head.

"Well, you certainly haven't given these Colorado girls a
break! Where's that Southern chivalry?"

Jim played Southern idiot. "Well, I just don't go out
much at all, I reckon."

"Just between us, neither do I. These girls here aren't
half as attractive as the ones back home." He winked and
Jim was disgusted. Although it was impossible for anyone in
the Army to be honest about such things, at least there were
more straightforward ways of going about a seduction. At
his present rate, it would take the sergeant weeks to come to

the point; probably just as well. Jim promised the sergeant that he would have dinner with him soon; then he excused himself and went back to the barracks, where he found a group of men sitting on his bunk. Most were clerks and not young; a bull session was in progress. Though Jim made a friendly motion, the men moved to other bunks. Jim took off his shirt and lay down. He said nothing. The bull session continued. As always, the dominant note was one of complaint. Apparently, each was losing an extraordinary amount of money while in the Army; and of course all officers were unjust and all women unfaithful.

Jim lay back on the coarse brown blanket and looked at the dark rafters. The barracks was always dark; there never seemed to be enough light or heat. He turned toward the coal stove and saw that there was a new man in the barracks, a young corporal, who sat on the bunk nearest the stove, listening politely, obviously aware that if a man wants to be accepted by a barracks, he must listen to a great deal of talk about a very few subjects, and he must accept as a law of nature that, whenever a point is made, it will be repeated a hundred times, often in the same words, rather like part-singing.

One of the more important sergeants (secretary to the personnel officer) was telling them about the general. "He's a real Section Eight case. Why, the other day he came into our office and he said to me, 'Sergeant,' he said, 'how many men've we got at Weatherley Field?' 'None,' I said, 'we lost them all to the fighter wing yesterday.' He didn't know that one of his own bases had been transferred the day before. Well, he tried to get out of it by saying he thought the transfer hadn't taken place yet. But that gives you some idea how his mind works, if it works. He's always thinking up ideas to discipline the men. As if we didn't have enough work running his wing for him. Didn't know about Weatherley being transferred!"

The others agreed that the general was too tough and not particularly bright. Or as another sergeant, whose past was mysterious with unspecified success, put it, "I'd like to see *him* hold down a job in civilian life. I'll bet he couldn't make thirty-five a week."

The others agreed solemnly that in their world the general would be far less than they, unable to make thirty-five a week.

Then the conversation turned to women.

Some liked plump women; some liked small women; some liked blondes, others brunettes, and a few liked red-haired women. But all were agreed that they liked women and as they talked their eyes brightened as they recalled wives, lovers, dreams. Jim was amused and puzzled: were these clerks really successful with women? None was attractive physically. They were either too fat or too thin, and he wondered how any woman could care for them. Yet they talked incessantly of conquests, boasting in order to impress other men who boasted—proof of what they said must be true. Even so, the thought of clerks in love was depressing.

Then one mentioned fairies. As far as Jim knew there were none in the barracks, except possibly the soldier who had started the conversation. He was small and round, with a flat unpleasant voice. "Just the other day this queer came up to me in the can in the movie house in town and wants me to go with him. Me! Well, I told the bastard what I thought of him. I told him if he didn't get out of there quick I'd break his neck, that's what I told him, and boy, he got out of there fast!" The others nodded solemnly when they heard this story, and each told an identical story, although in some instances the outraged man had indeed slugged the fairy. Jim tried not to laugh. It was always the ugliest and most suspect of the men who was invariably propositioned.

Jim glanced across at the young corporal. He was a dark-haired boy with gray eyes and a small slim body that looked strong. Watching him through half-closed eyes, Jim felt desire. For the first time in months he wanted sex. He wanted the young corporal. Mentally, he raped him, made love to him, worshiped him; they would be brothers and never parted.

"This town is full of those damn queers," the bald soldier droned on. "A guy can't be too careful." But since another conversation had started, no one except Jim heard. The soldier looked to Jim for support. "Isn't that right?"

"That's right," said Jim, continuing to look at the corporal, who yawned sleepily.

Jim was soon a friend of the corporal, whose name was Ken Woodrow, from Cleveland, aged twenty-one, in the Army a year and a half. He was a graduate of a secretarial college, and his ambition was to work for an important industrialist. Preferably in the Midwest, "where the people are real." Ken told him everything about himself and Jim listened intently, infatuated, unable to think of anything except how to get Ken to bed. Not since Bob had anyone so excited him. But with Bob there had been a sense of identity, of twins complementing one another; with Ken what he felt was absolute lust. He must have him.

They saw each other daily. Yet Ken seemed serenly unaware of what Jim wanted. Leading questions were invariably deflected by innocent answers. It was hugely frustrating. Meanwhile, Sergeant Kervinski observed them darkly and suspected the worst; he was particularly angry with Jim, who continued to refuse to have dinner with him in town.

At last, unable to bear the waiting another moment, Jim talked Ken into going with him to Colorado Springs. It was a sharp November night. They had an overnight pass. They would sleep at a hotel. Something would have to happen.

Colorado Springs was crowded with soldiers. They came not only from the air base but also from a neighboring infantry camp, crowding the streets, bars, movie theaters, poolrooms, bowling alleys, looking for sex and a good time.

Jim and Ken had dinner at an Italian restaurant. At the next table two pretty girls dined alone.

"See that girl staring at me?" Ken whispered, delighted. "You think we ought to ask them to join us?"

"Oh, no," said Jim as though the thought tired him. "I'm not up to it. I worked hard today. And I'm beat."

"Gosh, you never go out with girls, do you?" said Ken as though the thought had just occurred to him.

Jim had been waiting for this question for weeks. He had a lie ready. "Well, I got this one girl here in town, and I see her regularly, alone."

Ken nodded wisely. "See what you mean. Keep it to yourself. I figured you must have a setup like that, because you've been here quite a while and it wouldn't be natural not to have a chick somewhere." Ken nodded several times. They ate their spaghetti. Then Ken said, "She doesn't have any friends, does she? You know the kind I mean."

"Does who?"

"Your girl in town, does she . . . well, have friends?"

"Oh, no. At least I don't think so. That is, I'd have to ask her. She doesn't go out much."

"Well, where'd you meet her?"

Jim was irritated by the necessity to invent. "I met her at the USO, but like I told you she doesn't go out much. She works for the telephone company," he added, attempting verisimilitude.

"Oh." Ken was silent for a moment, his long fingers playing with a fork. "I met a girl last week. She was really stacked, and she had this apartment out by Pikes Peak. But I got so drunk I couldn't remember where it was when it was over, and she didn't tell me her name, so I don't know how to find her. Boy, I'd give anything to see that chick again. It's awful being in a town full of GIs and not knowing anybody."

"It's rough." Jim realized that he was getting nowhere. With each piece of new evidence, Ken's normality became more and more established. From the beginning, Jim had known that Ken was engaged to a girl in Cleveland, and that as soon as the war was over they would be married. But despite the engagement, Ken enjoyed talking about other girls and more than once he told Jim, solemnly, that he wondered if maybe he wasn't oversexed because he couldn't stop thinking about women. Since there was no evidence that Ken was interested in men, Jim's only hope was to trust in the ambivalence of a young man who liked him.

"Well," said Ken at last, eyes straying again to the two girls, "I guess we better go somewhere and get drunk, if you're sure you don't want to pick up something."

They toured the bars. Jim was careful not to get drunk. He had one drink for every two of Ken's. Wherever they went, Ken invariably struck up a conversation with a woman, but because Jim had said that he was tired Ken did not make a date for himself; he was going to be a "good buddy" and get drunk.

Shortly after midnight Ken was indeed very drunk, slurred speech, eyes glazed; he clung to the bar for support.

The moment had come. "Maybe we better stay in town tonight," said Jim.

"Sure, sure . . . good idea," mumbled Ken.

The night air was reviving. Jim helped Ken to walk without stumbling. They went to a hotel frequented by soldiers with overnight passes.

"Double bed or two singles?" asked the desk clerk.

"Which is cheapest?" asked Jim, who knew.

"Double." They registered. The room was like all other rooms in similar shabby hotels.

"Jeez, but I'm drunk." Ken stared at his own reflection in the mirror, face red, sweating, dark hair tangled over blood-shot eyes.

"So'm I." Jim watched him, wishing that he *was* drunk enough to do what he wanted to do.

"Jeez." Ken sat down on the large bed, which sagged in the middle. "I sure wish I had a date. I mean that I had a date with one of those girls we saw, and you had a date, too. That'd be something, wouldn't it? Four in a bed. I had a buddy once who liked to do that. He tried to get me to do that with him and a couple of girls, but not me, I like it private. I'd hate to have somebody watching, wouldn't you?"

"I sure would."

Ken stretched out on the bed, fully clothed, and shut his eyes. Jim shook him. He mumbled incoherently. Boldly Jim pulled off Ken's shoes, then the damp socks; Ken did not stir. But when he started to undo his belt, Ken opened his eyes and smiled; he looked like a corrupt choirboy. "Now that's what I call service," he said, wiggling his bare toes.

"I thought you'd passed out. Come on. Get your clothes off."

They both undressed down to their olive drab shorts.

Then Ken flung himself on the bed. "You sure sleep good when you're drunk," he said happily, and shut his eyes once more, and seemed to sleep.

Jim turned out the light. The darkness was complete. His heart beat rapidly. He was conscious of the warmth of Ken's body close to him. Slowly he moved his hand beneath the covers until he touched Ken's thigh; he waited, fingers resting lightly on the firm flesh.

Ken moved away. "Cut that out," he said in a clear sober voice.

A pulse beat furiously in Jim's temple. Blood rushed to his head. He turned over on his side. In the morning he would have a hangover.

III

THE WINTER WAS COLD and bitter. Snow came and went but the desert remained dry, and dust was forever in the wind. Jim was cold most of the time. During the day he spent as much time as he could in the hot sun, out of the wind. But at night he was always cold.

Neither Ken nor Jim acted as if anything untoward had happened, but Ken was plainly embarrassed, and Jim was furious. They avoided one another and now Jim found himself disliking the boy who had once filled his dreams with such intense passion. It was a lonely time. He had no friends. Even Sergeant Kervinski had proved fickle, transferring his affections to another physical-training instructor, newly arrived.

During the hard winter, Jim surrendered himself to an orgy of self-analysis. He thought continually about himself and his life and what it was that had made him the way he was. He pondered his early life.

Jim had disliked his father; he remembered that more clearly than anything else. His first memory was one of bleakness and unfair punishment. On the other hand he had liked his mother. Yet he found it strange that he could not recall her face although he could remember her voice: soft, Southern, tired. Far back in memory, he could recall a wonderful safe time when he was held in her arms while she kissed and fondled him. But all that ended when his brother was born, or so he supposed. She had never been demonstrative again.

School memories were vague. Jim had once been attracted to girls. When he was fourteen he was very interested in a heavy-breasted girl named Prudence. They exchanged valentines and the other children giggled that they were in love. He had sexual fantasies involving Prudence, but they stopped when he was fifteen and became interested in athletics and Bob. From that time on no one existed in the world except Bob.

Then came life at sea. He still shuddered when he remembered the night with Collins and the two girls in Seattle. He marveled now at how little he had understood then. Yet even now he wondered what might have happened if he had gone through with that adventure. He still half-believed that should he ever have a woman he would be normal. There was not much to base this hope on, but he believed it.

Memories of Shaw were pleasant and he smiled whenever he thought of him, despite the drama of their parting. He had learned much from Shaw; and through him he had met interesting people who might still be useful to him. Also, he found himself pitying Shaw, always a gratifying emotion, since it diminishes pleasurably the object.

Sullivan and Maria Verlaine were still too close to him for analysis. But he was aware that each had been important to him. Of the two he cared more for Maria, even though he now realized that he would never be able to make love to her, if only because they had talked too much about it. Words had taken the place of the act. Sullivan, too, had tended to vanish behind a screen of words, of emotions overstated yet undefined.

As for Bob, he had vanished. No one knew where he was, according to Mrs. Willard, who wrote Jim irregularly, giving him news of his father's illness, Carrie's marriage, John's admission to the State University. Yet Jim was positive that one day Bob would appear and they would continue what was begun that day beside the river. Until then, his life was in suspension, waiting.

Unable to bear the winter cold any longer, Jim went to Kervinski. He was at his desk, surrounded by the theatrical sergeants, soft young men who knew a thousand unpleasant stories about famous people.

"Well, Jim, what can I do for you?" Kervinski smiled brightly.

"I was wondering, Sergeant, if there's any chance of my going overseas."

Kervinski sighed. "Really, Jim, you don't know when you're well off. As it is, according to current orders, you'll be shipped out in April. But who knows? Anyway, there isn't a thing I or anybody can do. It's up to Washington."

"I was wondering if maybe I could get assigned to one of the bomber outfits they're forming here."

"Possibly. But they're not going overseas until spring. Anyway, why do you want to leave?"

"It's too goddamn cold. I'm freezing to death."

The sergeant laughed. "I'm afraid you'll just have to rough it with the rest of us. You Southern boys are so . . . sultry," he added, amusing the sergeants. That was that.

• • •

Christmas came and with it a blizzard. For two days wind and snow raged about the base. It was impossible to see more than a few feet in any direction. Men were lost going from building to building. Day was like night. When the blizzard stopped, the base had become a white lunar land with snowdrifts higher than buildings and craters that glittered in the sun.

In the club for enlisted men, a Christmas tree had been set up and the men gathered around it to drink beer and speak bitterly of past Christmases. Jim, bored, wandered over to the piano, where a corporal was picking out a tune with one finger. Not until Jim was at the piano did he realize that the corporal was Ken.

"Hello," said Jim. The moment was awkward.

"Hi." Ken was flat. "Kind of dull."

Jim nodded. "And I don't like beer."

"I remember. You been busy?" Ken continued his one-finger piano playing.

"Just trying to keep warm."

"I thought you were in Alaska once."

"But since then I was in the tropics too long. I hate cold weather."

"Why don't you transfer to Louisiana? We got a new base there."

"How?"

Ken was now playing the Marine Corps Hymn. "Well, if you want me to, I can fix it up with the sergeant in personnel. He's a good buddy of mine."

"I wish you would."

"I'll ask him tomorrow."

"Thanks." Jim was grateful, also suspicious. Why was Ken so willing to help? Did he want him to leave Colorado?

The next day, by accident, Jim met Sergeant Kervinski in the post library. The sergeant was reading a movie magazine.

"Hello, Jim." Kervinski blushed. "I expect we're both goldbricks today. By the way, Ken told me he spoke to you about Louisiana."

"That's right." Jim was startled. "I didn't know you knew him."

"Oh, yes!" Kervinski beamed. "As a matter of fact, we're going into the Springs for dinner tonight. Why don't you join us?" The invitation was put in such a way that it was perfectly clear that the last thing in the world Kervinski wanted was for Jim to join them.

"No, thanks. Not tonight. He's a good guy, Ken."

"I think so. I first noticed him when you and he used to go around together when he first arrived, remember? Such a sincere person."

"Yes." Jim was suddenly angry. "Yes, he's OK." He paused, searching for a way to wound his successor. The best he could do was "I guess Ken's going to be married soon."

Kervinski was serene. "Oh, I don't think there's any *immediate* danger. He's having too good a time. Besides, it's a lot cheaper to buy milk than keep a cow."

Jim looked at Kervinski with perfect loathing. But the sergeant gave no sign that he was aware of Jim's dislike. "You know that we'll be shipping quite a few men down to Louisiana."

Jim got the point at last. "Yes, Ken's going to see if I can be one of them. Do you think it'll be all right with Captain Banks?"

"Of course it'll be all right. We'd hate to lose you, naturally." Jim was baffled. He had failed with Ken. Kervinski had been successful. It seemed impossible, yet obviously something had happened and both were now eager for Jim to be shipped out.

"Thanks," said Jim, and left the library, contemplating murder.

But Jim was not transferred to Louisiana. On New Year's Day he caught a chill. He went to the hospital and was put to bed, with a streptococcic infection of the throat. For several days he was delirious, tortured by memory, by certain words and phrases which repeated themselves until he swore aloud and twisted in his bed. He dreamed of Bob, of a menacing, subtly distorted Bob who retreated when he tried to touch him. Sometimes the river was between them, and when he tried to swim across, he would be dashed against sharp rocks, Bob's derisive laughter ringing in his ears.

Then he would hear the voice of Shaw talking and talking and talking of love, saying the same things in the same way, until Jim knew how each sentence would end by its first word; yet there was no way of silencing the voice; it was literally maddening.

Then there were memories of his mother, holding him in her arms, the face no longer gray and lined but young, the way she had been when he was a child and secure. Then his father would approach and he would slip from her arms and his father would beat him, while the river roared in his ears.

The pain in his throat was sharp, like a knife blade probing, underscoring his nightmares. He remained in this dream-haunted state for what seemed years. But on the third day, chronologically, the fever broke and the dreams ended, and he woke up one morning, tired and weak; the worst was over.

Jim was in a small room in the base hospital. Through the window he could see snowy mountains. He was conscious of being quite alone and for a moment he wondered if he might not be the only person left in the world, but then the muffled sound of voices reassured him and the nurse entered the room.

"I see we're better today." She took his pulse and put a thermometer in his mouth. "You know, you were quite sick for a while there." Her tone was accusing, as she removed the thermometer from his mouth. "Normal at last. Well, we stuffed enough sulfa into you."

"How long've I been here?" Jim's voice was weak; it hurt him to talk.

"This is your third day, and don't talk. The doctor will be around soon." She put a glass of water beside his bed and left.

The doctor was cheerful. He examined Jim's throat and nodded with satisfaction. "Good. Good. You'll be out of here in a few weeks."

Apparently Jim had nearly died. This did not surprise him. There had been times in his delirium when he would have been glad to depart. "Anyway, it's over now. But it may be weeks before you can go back to active duty."

The days passed quickly and pleasantly. It was the most comfortable period of Jim's Army career. He read magazines and listened to the radio. In time he was transferred to a ward with twenty other convalescents. He was perfectly content with life, until the pains began, first in his left knee, then in his left shoulder, a constant aching, like a bad tooth. After a number of tests, the doctor sat on Jim's bed and talked to him in a low voice while the others in the ward tried to hear.

"Are you absolutely certain that you've never had these pains before?"

"No, sir, never." Jim had been asked this particular question a dozen times.

"Well, I'm afraid that you've got what we call rheumatoid arthritis." He sighed. "Contracted while in the Army."

The ward boy had already given Jim the same diagnosis and so he was prepared for the verdict. Even so, he managed to look alarmed. "Is that bad, sir?"

"Not in this stage, no. It'll be painful, of course. Not that we know much about arthritis, though I'm willing to bet your throat infection had something to do with it. Meanwhile, you'll be sent to a warm, dry climate. Does no good, of course, but it'll make you feel better. Then they'll probably discharge you with a pension, because the calcium deposits show up in the X rays, and it all happened to you while serving your country in time of war, and you've got a swell racket from here on out."

"Where will I be sent, sir?"

"California desert, maybe Arkansas, Arizona. We'll let you know." The doctor stood up slowly. "I've got the same thing as you." He chuckled. "Maybe they'll discharge me, too." He left, and Jim wondered if there was anyone in the world he liked so much as this particular doctor.

"You going to be shipped out?" asked the Negro soldier in the bunk next to his.

Jim nodded, hiding his great happiness.

"Man, you're lucky. I'd sure like to be shipped out of here, to anywhere."

"It's tough."

The Negro then talked about intolerance and discrimination. He was certain that even if he were dying the white officers would not take proper care of him. To cite an example, he told a long rambling story about a Negro soldier who had gone to an Army doctor a number of times for backache and the doctor had told him that there was nothing wrong with him. One day when the soldier was sitting in the waiting room and the nurse went in to tell the doctor that he was there, he heard the doctor say distinctly, "Well, send the nigger in." White doctors were racially intolerant. Everyone knew it. But someday . . .

As the Negro talked about the miseries of his race, Jim thought only of his own happiness. He had long since given up all idea of going overseas. From the stories he had heard it was hardly more exciting than duty in the States. He was now eager to leave the Army. He had been no use at all to the war. Soon he would be free. Meanwhile the thought of his pending release made him want to resume relations with those who had been important to him. He borrowed writing paper from the Negro soldier and slowly, laboriously, in his awkward, childish handwriting, he began to write letters, using them as a net in order to recapture his own past.

CHAPTER
8

RONALD SHAW WAS TIRED and there was an uncomfortable pain in his duodenum which he was convinced was an ulcer, if not cancer. His death took place before his eyes, beautifully lit and photographed, with Brahms playing on the sound track. Then there was a slow dissolve to the funeral cortege as it moved through Beverly Hills, escorted by weeping girls carrying autograph books.

Tears in his eyes, Shaw turned into the green oasis of Bel Air. It had been a bad day at the studio. He disliked his new director and he hated the part he was playing. For the first time he was supporting a woman star. He wished now that he had turned down the part, or at least had it rewritten, or retired from the screen before he died of overwork and cancer. The bright cheerful sun made things worse; his head ached; perhaps he was going to have sunstroke.

But the house was cool and he gave a weak sigh of relief as the butler held the door open for him.

"A bad day, sir?" The butler was sympathetic.

"Terrible." Shaw picked up his mail and went out to the swimming pool, where George was taking a sunbath. George was a sailor from Wisconsin with hair so blond that it was white. He had been with Shaw for a week. In another week he would go back to sea. Then what? Shaw asked himself bitterly.

"Hi, Ronnie." The boy pulled himself up on one elbow. "How's the salt mine?"

"Rotten." Shaw sat down beside the pool. "The director's an untalented, lousy, professional kike." Shaw had begun lately to make anti-Semitic remarks, which amused rather than distressed those who knew him.

"I guess they're pretty lousy, some of them out here." George was a happy youth who believed everything that he was told. Shaw tousled the blond hair idly. They had met in a bar in Hollywood. Shaw had started to frequent bars, a dangerous pastime, but he was bored and restless, and morbidly aware of time passing, and of the fact that his hair was quite gray beneath the dye and that his stomach was bad, and life was ending even though he was hardly forty. Why? Too much had happened to him, he decided; his career had burned him up and of course he had been unfortunate in love, cheated and betrayed.

George stretched out again beside the pool while Shaw read his mail. He opened Jim's letter. The handwriting was unfamiliar and at first he thought it was a fan letter. Then he saw that it was signed quite formally, "Jim Willard." Shaw was pleased, flattered, suspicious: if Jim wanted money, he would not get it. That would be Shaw's revenge as well as a good lesson for Jim, who had deserted a truly genuine human being for a self-centered writer. Shaw was slightly disappointed to find that the letter was friendly and nothing more.

Jim wrote that he was in the Army hospital but no longer sick. He expected to be discharged soon and he would like to see Shaw again. It was puzzling and yet in character. Jim had always been direct. Shaw experienced a sudden ache of sexual memory. Then he saw that George was watching him. "What you got?" asked George. "A fan letter?"

Shaw smiled dreamily. "No, it's from a kid I used to know, Jim Willard. I showed you his picture once."

"What happened to him?"

"He went into the Army," Shaw lied glibly. "He writes me often. I suppose he's still in love with me, at least that's what he says. But I don't feel anything anymore. Funny, isn't it?"

George nodded, impressed. Then Shaw sent him into the pavilion for a drink. As the late afternoon sun shone in Shaw's face and a soft flower-scented wind cooled him, his unhappiness turned to a detachment that was not at all unpleasant. He was utterly alone in the world. This knowledge thrilled him. Of course there was his mother in Baltimore and a few friends at the studio, as well as the millions who knew of him and would doubtless be honored to be his friend; yet having conquered all the world, he was still very much alone and it struck him that there was something magnificent in being a prisoner of fame. He allowed a brooding look to come into his eyes. What a waste, he thought, contemplating the inability of others to reciprocate the love he had to give. None could equal his intensity. A tragic figure, he sat with the western sun in his eyes, perfectly content.

George approached with two glasses. "Here you go." He gave Shaw his drink.

Shaw thanked him very gently.

"You feeling OK, Ronnie?"

"Oh, yes, thank you." The gin was cold. Suddenly a

spasm went through his stomach. For an instant he was panicky. But then he belched and the pain went away: it was only gas.

Mr. Willard was dying and Mrs. Willard wished that he would die soon. Apparently years of bad temper had damaged his liver and weakened his heart. The doctors were able to keep him from pain with great doses of morphine.

Mrs. Willard grimaced as she entered the sickroom; the odor of medicines and dying was overpowering. Mr. Willard lay on his back, breathing noisily. His face was yellow and sagging and the once-commanding mouth hung loose. His eyes were like gray glass from the morphine.

"That you, Bess?" His voice was hoarse.

"Yes, dear. How're you feeling?" She arranged the pillows.

"Better. The doctor said I was better." The evening before, the doctor had told Mrs. Willard that her husband would not live another week.

"I know, he told me the same."

"I'll be up and around soon." Mr. Willard would not admit to himself that he was going to die. He asked his wife about the courthouse.

"They're doing fine, dear. Mr. Perkins is doing your job until you're ready to go back to work."

"Perkins is an ass," said Mr. Willard.

"I'm sure he's doing his best. After all, he's only filling in."

Mr. Willard grunted and shut his eyes. Dispassionately his wife looked at the sunken yellow face, and wondered where the insurance policy was. She had not been able to find it anywhere in the house, but of course the will would tell, and the will was at the lawyer's office. Mr. Willard's eyes shut, and he seemed to sleep. She left the room.

On the floor in the hall were several letters. As she leaned over to pick them up, she groaned. The older she got, the more she disliked bending over. But then she forgot her pains: one of the letters was from Jim.

She read it slowly. He was in the hospital and that alarmed her, but he reassured her that he was now well and would soon be getting out of the Army. He promised to come home and visit her as soon as he was free. Her heart beat more quickly as she read this.

She thought of her older son, and wondered what she felt about him after such a long separation, much of it without communication of any sort.

She had not wanted him to leave home. She had wept the night he left even though she realized that he could never live in the same house with his father. In her quiet way, Mrs. Willard had hated her husband from the first day of their marriage. During family quarrels, she had sympathized with Jim and longed to tell him that she felt as he did but that they both had to bear those things which could not be changed. Unfortunately, she had never spoken frankly, and because she had not, Jim left home. Now, of course, it was too late. Jim would never belong to her again. She wanted to cry but she could not.

Mrs. Willard sat erect, the letter in her hands, wondering what had happened to her life. Soon she would be alone, without even a husband to hate in the last years of her life. Where had all the time and all the promise gone to? She pitied herself, but only for a moment. After all, Carrie and her husband lived nearby and so would John once he was a lawyer.

The thought of Jim's return cheered her considerably. She wondered how he looked now that he was a man. She had no clue except the photograph in the movie magazine which she had shown to everyone, creating an impression that Jim was a movie star, an impression she had never entirely corrected.

Mrs. Willard daydreamed pleasantly of the future. There were several nice girls who would make Jim the kind of wife who would be glad to share him with his mother. As for a job, Jim could take over the physical-training post at the high school. She knew enough politicians to make this possible. Yes, the future could be good, she decided, putting the letter away and returning to the sickroom to find that her husband's eyes were open. He was staring at the ceiling.

"I've a letter from Jim."

"What does he say?"

"He's been in the hospital—it's not serious—and he thinks he'll be discharged from the Army soon. Then he'll come home."

"Probably broke." Mr. Willard scowled briefly; his features were too weak to hold even a scowl for long. "Wonder what he'll do when he gets out? Can't go on playing games forever."

"I thought perhaps he could get a job at the high school. I . . . we could get him something, don't you think? I'm sure Judge Claypoole would be glad to arrange it."

Mr. Willard's skeleton hands fumbled with the white sheet. "How old's the boy now?"

Mrs. Willard thought a moment. "Twenty-two come April."

"He's grown." Mr. Willard was gloomy.

"Yes," said Mrs. Willard happily. Jim would take care of her. "He's grown."

"Don't know why he wants to wander all over."

"But the experience is good for him and anyway you know what they say about wild oats."

Mr. Willard shut his eyes. Conversation tired him. Mrs. Willard went to the kitchen, where she found Carrie. "How is he, Mother?"

"It's almost over. A few more days at the most. Thank the Lord he feels no pain."

"That's something to be grateful for." Of them all, Carrie was the only one truly sorry about her father's approaching death. They had been fond of one another. But her sorrow was somewhat assuaged by the fact of pregnancy. Inclined to plumpness, Carrie was now round and contented and looked to be exactly what she was, a comfortable housewife fond of her husband. Mrs. Willard gave Carrie Jim's letter.

Carrie was delighted. "I do hope he comes back and lives here!"

"So do I."

"I wonder what he's like now."

"We'll know when we see him. Now I expect you better go in and see Father."

Carrie left the kitchen and Mrs. Willard began to fix broth for her husband. It would be a great relief to her when he died. She wondered idly if he might not have left the insurance policy with his friend Judge Claypoole. But of course the will would tell them everything.

London was chilly and damp and Sullivan was depressed as he walked past St. James's Palace on the way to his hotel in Mount Street.

He had been to dinner with H. G. Wells, whom he admired as a figure if not as a writer. The evening had gone well; Mr. Wells had been in good form. Yet Sullivan was

obscurely irritated by the perfectly plain fact that not only
had the great man never read one of Sullivan's books, he
had never heard of him either. Naturally Wells was an old
man but even so it was disquieting and Sullivan was again
reminded of his literary failure.

The night was dark and the blackout made it even darker.
A cold wind blew through the streets. Shivering, he fastened
his trench coat at the neck. He would have a strong drink
when he got back to the hotel bar, even if it meant running
into Amelia, who was now in London. Aggressive, bustling,
eager for bygones to be bygones, his ex-wife was unbearably
cheery.

And of course there she was, thin and untidy, enthroned
in the hotel bar, surrounded by correspondents (she herself
was covering the war for a left-wing magazine).

"Paul dear, come on over!" He did.

The other correspondents greeted Sullivan respectfully.
At least they knew he was an author. They were impressed
by novelists, though they did not take his journalism very
seriously, for which he could hardly blame them.

Sullivan shook hands all around. He knew most of them
by reputation. Those who were not Stalinists were crypto-
Trotskyites. Sullivan was apolitical. But Amelia was totally
engaged. She talked rapidly, maintaining herself as group
leader. "Paul's such a dear. Really, I always think one should
be nice to one's ex-husbands, don't you?" The question was
asked at large and no one answered. "I believe if we're to be
really civilized we should have no bitterness when we fail at
marriage or anything else, except perhaps politics." She was
a little drunk. "Does that sound like that lovable old cynic
La Rochefoucauld? Everything else does!" She laughed
gaily, then turned to Sullivan. "Where've you been this
evening?"

"I had dinner with H. G. Wells." Sullivan won that round. Immediately everyone asked him about Wells and for a moment Amelia ceased to be the center; even when she loudly demanded a drink for her ex-husband, he still retained his lead. "He was very pleasant. We talked about writing mostly. He'd read one of my books and so I was quite flattered by that. Not that I supposed he liked it, but even so . . ."

"Here's your drink, Paul." Amelia thrust the whiskey at him. He took a swallow and Amelia filled the brief silence. "I think," she said to the table at large, "that it will be years before there is a Labour government in England. The Churchill-Cliveden set are too well entrenched and, just between us, I shouldn't be in the least surprised if they created some sort of dictatorship that could *never* be thrown off without a revolution, and you know how slow these English are at revolting against anything! A nation of masochists."

Paul was surprised to find that people took Amelia seriously. He could hardly be critical; he had married her. But when they first met she was different. A quiet, thoughtful girl, she had worshiped him until it was plain that a physical relationship was impossible. Then, defensively, she had grown masculine and aggressive. It was all his fault, he decided, or at least the fault of the way he was, and this racketing woman was the result. Did nothing turn out well?

Sullivan finished his drink and stood up. "If you'll excuse me, Amelia, I must cut class." Though he said this amiably enough, he was pleased to see that he still had the power to hurt her. She stopped in midsentence: the needle had been lifted from the record. He said good night to the correspondents and left the bar. As he entered the lobby, he could hear Amelia beginning again.

At the desk Sullivan got his mail and took the lift to his room, hoping there would be no air-raid warning to break his sleep. He was weary. Not until he was in bed did he notice Jim's letter on the night table. He read the letter twice and was both disappointed and pleased. Jim was going to be discharged from the Army and he would like to see him again. Nothing more. No mention of Maria. Did that mean their affair would continue, if it was an affair? During the months Sullivan had been in England, he had thought of Jim often, dreamed of him, wanted him. Could they resume? That was the question.

It was morning before Sullivan fell asleep. During the long night he thought mostly of the books he had written, and he was filled with gloom. He had succeeded at nothing. He had no lover, no family, and H. G. Wells had never heard of him. But then as he grew sleepy, he comforted himself. After all, he was young and there was still time left in which to write a masterpiece, as well as to recapture Jim. Meanwhile, first thing in the morning, he would send Mr. Wells one of his novels, autographed.

Jim's letter made Maria Verlaine sad and somewhat embarrassed. She had been a fool to love a child incapable of response. She had deserved to suffer, and she had, for a time. Now she wanted only normal men and uncomplicated attachments.

In New York, despite the austerities of wartime, she dined out often, met strangers, made love. In constant motion, she ceased to think of herself as a tragic figure. Now this unexpected letter reminded her of that strangely lowering season she had spent in Yucatán with a boy and his lover. Did she want to see him again? She thought not. She was at an age when she did not care to be reminded of old defeats. Yet at the same time she was sorry for Jim. More to the point, was it not a proof of her own power that he had again turned to her? and of her own maturity that she could receive him as a friend? Yes, she would write to him. They would meet when he came to New York. After all, she had nothing to fear, nothing to gain. The worst had happened.

Everyone agreed that Bob Ford looked remarkably handsome in his Merchant Marine uniform. First mate aboard a Liberty ship, of all the hometown youths at war, he was considered the most successful. Of course, the Merchant Marine was not exactly the Army or Navy, but still it was quite an achievement to be a first mate and not yet twenty-five. His homecoming was something of a triumph, although, properly speaking, he had no home since his father had been committed to the insane asylum the year before, and the family home was now a boardinghouse. The new owner, however, was willing to rent him his old room at half price, and here he stayed during the two weeks of his leave, while he wooed Sally Mergendahl, the reason for his return. They had written one another for five years. During that time, Sally had grown into a quiet pretty woman, no longer "wild." As a child, she had made up her mind that she was going to marry Bob, and nothing had ever caused her to change her mind. Now her patience was rewarded. One evening, while walking her home from the movies, Bob spoke of marriage.

"Are you sure that you really *want* to be married? Could you be married and still be a sailor?"

Bob looked at her. They were standing beneath a tall elm tree; his face was in darkness, hers in the light from a nearby streetlamp.

"I'm sure I want to marry you. But I love the sea. It's the only thing I know."

"I talked to Daddy," said Sally slowly, "and he thought you would do very well in the insurance business, in his business, and he thought it was a shame that someone with your personality was away at sea all the time when you could be in business with him, selling insurance, as a partner."

"You think he'd give me a job after the war?"

Sally nodded. She had already won that battle.

"Then if it's all right with you, let's get married right away."

"I think," said Sally Mergendahl, "that that would be a very good idea."

The morning of the wedding was a Sunday. Church bells rang, and most people slept an hour late. But Bob was up early. He shaved carefully, put on his newest uniform, and went downstairs for breakfast. His landlady was ecstatic.

"What a lovely day for a wedding! Though any day's a good day to get married. I made pancakes. There's nothing like a full stomach to start you off with. Oh, by the way, here's a letter for you. It came Friday, but in the excitement I forgot all about giving it to you. I'm sorry. It was addressed to you in care of old Mr. Ford here, which means it's from somebody out of town. Well, enjoy your breakfast. I'll see you at the church. I wouldn't miss this for anything!"

Bob opened Jim's letter. He was surprised to hear from him after so many years; he also felt a bit guilty for not having answered those early letters Jim had written him. Sally occupied what little talent he had for correspondence.

The letter was simple enough. Jim was getting out of the

service and he hoped to see Bob soon, perhaps in New York. That was all. Something disturbed Bob as he crumpled the letter. He frowned and tried to remember what it was. But his mind was a blank. As he tossed the letter neatly into a wastebasket, he made a vow that he would answer Jim's letter the moment he got back to ship.

CHAPTER
9

I

JIM WAS NOT DISCHARGED immediately. Instead he was sent
to a hospital in the San Fernando Valley of California,
where he was treated and observed. In the hot sun his
arthritic condition improved but, because he was now eager
to get out of the Army, he said nothing of this to the
doctors. He continued to limp in a most distinguished way.

Jim visited Hollywood often, but he did not go to see
Shaw since he had received no answer to his letter; he
assumed that Shaw was still living with Peter and not interested in a reconciliation. But he did meet the director
named Cy, in a bar, sitting too close to a sailor, drunk.
When Cy saw Jim he shouted, "Well, if it isn't the tennis
boy!" He was exuberant. "So what's new? In that butch
uniform yet! Been to see America's Sweetheart?"

"No. Not yet."

"Where you stationed?"

Jim told him.

"A hospital? What's wrong? A rosy chancre? The dread disease that dare not tell its name?"

"No, arthritis."

"Serious?"

"Not very."

"Well, let's have a drink."

Jim shook his head. "I'm not drinking."

"Then I'll have one." Cy ordered himself gin. "So why haven't you been to see Shaw?"

"Because I don't think he wants to see me, do you?"

Cy took a swallow of his new drink and wiped his mouth with a hairy paw. "Oh, you know Shaw. He's such a ham. Who was the one who came after you? I've forgotten."

"Peter, an actor."

"That one!" Cy beamed with malice. "Well, I'm responsible for that breakup. In a way. I put the kid in a picture and, believe it or not, he was good. So the studio offers him a term contract, he takes it, and walks out on Shaw, who, by the way, got me to put him in the picture in the first place. Isn't that a hoot? But hell, I don't blame the kid. After all, he wasn't even queer. He's shacked up with a broad at this very moment, at Malibu. Saw them myself this afternoon, on the beach."

"Who's with Shaw now?" The story of Peter was not entirely surprising.

"Everybody. Nobody. He hunts the bars and the studio is worried as all hell. And . . . oh, by the way, he's going in the Navy. Now that's a *real* hoot!"

"But I thought he was supposed to be too valuable or something to go."

Cy chuckled. "You got to go to war if you want to make

154 ▲ GORE VIDAL

pictures. He'll be commissioned and sent overseas to maybe Honolulu and we'll take a lot of pictures of him being one of the boys and then, if the Navy doesn't lock him up for raping their personnel, he'll come home with a couple of ribbons and a new contract from the studio. Last few months they've been working him hard, so there'll be plenty of Shaw pictures while he's gone. The idiots won't be allowed to forget him."

"When's he going in?"

"As soon as the Navy gets the go-ahead from *Life*."

"Nice deal," said Jim. The bartender began to move ominously toward him: nondrinkers were unpopular. "Well, I'll see you around."

"Why don't you come on up to my place tonight . . ." Cy began.

"No, thanks."

"Suit yourself."

The routine of the hospital was a relief after Colorado, and Jim enjoyed himself. He played tennis for the first time in two years. He gained weight and soon his illness was a barely remembered nightmare, like the cold white mornings on the Colorado desert.

In April his mother wrote to tell him that his father had died. Jim felt no regret. Almost the contrary: a weight was lifted in his mind, a hatred ended. Jim sat in the sun and looked across the green lawn, where patients in maroon Army dressing gowns were wandering back and forth.

Death seemed impossible in the sunlight. Yet Jim wondered what it was like. He himself had been close to death but he could recall nothing. Now, in the sunlight, he pondered death and his father. He did not believe in heaven or hell. He thought it most unlikely that there was a special place where good people went, particularly when no one was certain just what a good person was, much less what the final repository was like. What *did* happen? The idea of nothing frightened him, and death was probably nothing: no earth, no people, no light, no time, no *thing*. Jim looked at his hand. It was tanned and square, and covered with fine gold hairs. He imagined the hand as it would be when he was dead: limp, pale, turning to earth. He stared for a long time at the hand which was certain to be earth one day. Decay and nothing, yes, that was the future. He was chilled by a cold animal fear. There must be some way to cheat the earth, which like an inexorable magnet drew men back to it. But despite the struggle of ten thousand generations, the magnet was triumphant, and sooner or later his own particular memories would be spilled upon the ground. Of course his dust would be absorbed in other living things and to that degree at least he would exist again, though it was plain enough that the specific combination which was he would never exist again.

The hot sun warmed him. The blood moved fast in his veins. He was conscious of the fullness of life. He existed in the present. That was enough. And perhaps in the years ahead he would have a new vision, one which would help him, somehow, to circumvent the fact of nothing.

In May Jim went before the medical board. Since X rays showed a mineral deposit in his left knee joint, it was the decision of the board that James Willard be medically discharged from the Army of the United States, with a pension for disability. To his delight, all this came to pass. Papers at last in order, he was given a railroad ticket to New York. On the train he read in a newspaper that Ronald Shaw, the actor, had enlisted in the Navy.

• • •

In New York Jim rented a room on Charles Street in Greenwich Village and looked for work. After some time he found what he wanted. Near the East River there was a vacant lot which had been converted to tennis courts. Here Jim met Wilbur Gray, who, with his partner Isaac Globe, owned the courts. Eventually a new building would go up on the lot but, according to Mr. Globe, that was at least five years away, and in the meantime, business was excellent.

Jim visited the courts every day. He became friends with both Gray and Globe. Finally, he offered to buy part of their business and to be an instructor as well. After many conferences and much examining of books, the men, who knew nothing about tennis, agreed to allow Jim, who knew nothing about business, to become their partner.

Jim worked for the rest of the year, giving lessons on good days, and since there were an unusual number of good days that summer and fall, he made money. Outside of work, he saw very little of his partners. They were both devoted family men and had no interest in the outside world. Neither did he while he was working. He saw no one. He did call Maria Verlaine's hotel once, but she was not registered.

One winter afternoon, on Fifth Avenue, Jim saw Lieutenant Shaw, looking rather wistfully at a display of Christmas toys in the window of F.A.O. Schwarz's.

"Ronnie!"

"Jim!" They shook hands warmly. Shaw had been at sea in the Atlantic. He was now on leave, living at the Harding Hotel. Would Jim like a drink? Yes.

The suite in the Harding was vast, with rococo mirrors and spindly gold-encrusted furniture. Shaw ordered a bottle of Scotch and then they stared at one another, each wondering how to begin. At last Shaw remarked that a lot of water had gone under the bridge since they last met. Jim agreed. Then the conversation stopped for a long time until Shaw said, "Are you living alone?"

Jim nodded. "I worked pretty hard all summer; I don't really know anybody yet."

"You're better off playing the field. I know I am. Ideally, of course, a relationship is best, but then how many people are capable of deep feeling? Practically none."

Jim put an end to that familiar dirge. "How's the Navy?"

Shaw shrugged. "I've had to be careful. But then I've always had to be careful. By the way, what're you doing tonight? I've been invited to a faggot party, very chichi. I'll take you. It can be your coming-out party in New York. They'll all be there."

Jim was surprised at how little Shaw seemed to care for appearances. In the old days he would never have gone to such a party. But now he was indifferent, even defiant.

The party was given by Nicholas J. Rolloson, heir to a notorious American fortune. Rolly, as he was known, had two passions, modern art and the military. Both were well represented in his apartment overlooking Central Park. Paintings by Chagall and Dufy hung on stark white walls. Mobiles tinkled from the ceiling. A huge Henry Moore nude dominated one end of a long drawing room in which at least one chair resembled a wrecked armadillo. Through these startling rooms a full company of soldiers, sailors, and marines wandered, awed by their surroundings if not by Rolly and his friends, who were perfectly familiar to them.

There was a hush when Shaw entered. Although there were other famous men at the party—painters, writers, composers, athletes, even a member of Congress—Shaw was most glamorous of all. Eyes watched his every move. He was a legend here, and that made him entirely happy.

Rolly welcomed them enthusiastically; he wore a scarlet blazer with a crest. As he moved, breasts jiggled beneath a pale yellow silk shirt. The handshake was predictably damp. "My dears, how lovely of you to come! I was so afraid you wouldn't, Ronnie, and I would have died of disappointment, but now my evening is made, but absolutely *made*! Now come with me. Everybody's just about out of their minds to meet you." Shaw was borne away, and Jim was left on his own. A waiter gave him a martini. Cocktail in hand, Jim went exploring, somewhat excited by the servicemen, conscripts in Rolloson's army.

In a corner of the dining room, Jim was hailed by an effeminate man with a hairpiece. "Come on over, baby. Join the party." Without alternative, Jim sat down on the couch between the hairpiece and a set of bifocals. Opposite sat a gray-haired man and a bald young man. They had been talking earnestly and both the gray-haired man and the bifocals were irritated at being interrupted.

"You came with Shaw, didn't you?" asked the hairpiece.

Jim nodded.

"Are you an actor?"

"A tennis player." Jim ground out the phrase in his deepest voice.

"Oh, how thrilling! An athlete! I adore body men," said the bifocals. "Teutonic and primitive, not like those of us who are simply frustrated and inhibited by a society grown too complex to understand. This young man is the true archetype, the original pattern of which we are neurotic distortions." The bifocals examined Jim as if he were some sort of moderately interesting experiment.

The gray-haired man objected. "Why are the rest of us necessarily the result of a distortion? In any case, you are being taken in by an appearance. We don't know his reality. He could be most neurotic of all. By the way"—he turned to Jim with a smile—"we speak of you not as yourself but as a symbol. We're not being impertinent."

"But there is something," said the bald man, "in this Teutonic theory. In Germany, isn't it the army, the athletes, the most virile men, who are homosexual, or at least bisexual? And God knows Germany is primitive enough. On the other hand, in America and in England we find that effeminacy is one of the signs of the homosexual, and of course neurosis."

"Five years ago we might have thought that true," said bifocals. "But I'm not so sure now. Of course there have always been normal-appearing men who were homosexual but never or seldom practiced, while the other type (what you call Teutonic) was not so much in evidence and we knew very little about them and thought they were just trade, you know, the truck driver who enjoyed being had but pretended that he was really interested in women and money. But I think the war has caused a great change. Inhibitions have broken down. All sorts of young men are trying out all sorts of new things, away from home and familiar taboos."

"Everyone is by nature bisexual," said the gray-haired man. "Society, early conditioning, good or bad luck—depending on how you were told to look at it—determine the result. Nothing is 'right.' Only denial of instinct is wrong."

Across the room, Shaw motioned for Jim to join him. Jim excused himself.

Shaw and Rolly were surrounded by sailors, who regarded Jim jealously as he joined them.

"I thought you looked bored with those intellectuals," said Shaw.

"Who were they?" asked Jim.

"Well, the gray-haired one is a professor at City College

and the one with glasses is a journalist—you'd know his name if I could remember it—and the other one is a perfect bitch," said Rolly, patting his thick lustrous hair. "They were probably talking politics. So dreary! I say, why worry? Let them eat cake and all that sort of thing. I mean, after all, really, isn't live and let live the best policy?"

Jim agreed that indeed it was and Rolly pinched his thigh. Shaw was suddenly carried off by the sailors and Jim was left with Rolly, trapped.

"I understand from Ronnie that you're a tennis player. Now I think that's terribly exciting . . . I mean to be an athlete and work out of doors. I've always thought that if I had my life to live over, which fortunately I haven't, I would have spent more time alfresco, doing things. As it is, I do nothing. You know I do nothing, don't you? I hope you don't hate me. Everyone's so snobbish about working these days. It's the Communists, they're everywhere, saying people must *produce*. Well, I say that there must be somebody who knows how to appreciate *what's* produced. Which is why I'm really quite a *useful* member of society. After all I keep money in circulation and other people get it and I do so believe in everyone having a good time. . . . Oh, there's that butch Marine, isn't he something? He was had five times last Sunday and still went to Mass, so he told me." Jim looked at this celebrity, who turned out to be a rather tired-looking young man in uniform.

"You know, I loathe these screaming pansies," said Rolly, twisting an emerald and ruby ring. "I have a perfect weakness for men who are butch. I mean, after all, why be a queen if you like other queens, if you follow me? Luckily, nowadays everybody's *gay*, if you know what I mean . . . *literally* everybody! So different when I was a girl. Why, just a few days ago a friend of mine . . . well, I wouldn't go so far as to say a *friend*, actually I think he's rather *sinister*, but anyway this acquaintance was actually keeping Will Jepson, the *boxer*! Now, I mean, really, when things get that far, things have really gone far!"

Jim agreed that things had indeed gone far. Rolly rather revolted him, but he recognized that he meant to be kind and that was a good deal.

"My, isn't it crowded in here? I love for people to enjoy themselves! I mean the right kind of people who appreciate this sort of thing. You see, I've become a Catholic."

Jim took this information in stride.

"It started with Monsignor Sheen, those *blue eyes*! But of course I needed Faith. I had to know just where I'm going when I shuffle off this mortal thing, and the Catholic Church is *so* lovely, with that *cozy* grandeur that I adore. One feels so *safe* with the rituals and everything and those robes! Well, there just isn't *anything* to compare with them. They have *really* the most beautiful ceremonies in the world. I was in St. Peter's once for Easter—I think it was Easter—anyway, the Holy Father came riding in on a golden throne wearing the triple tiara and the most beautiful white robes you've ever seen and the cardinals all in red and the incense and the beautiful marble and gold statues . . . absolutely *yummy*! Anyway, then and there I became a Catholic. I remember turning to Dario Alarimo (he was a dear friend of mine of an extremely old Neapolitan family, his father was a duke and he would have been a duke, too, but I believe he was killed in the war because he was a Fascist, though all the best people were Fascists in those days, even though we all realized that Mussolini was hardly chic). What was I talking about? I was about to make a point. Oh, yes, about becoming a Catholic. So I turned to Dario and I said, 'This is the most splendid thing I've ever seen,' and he turned to me and said, 'Isn't it, Rolly?' All my friends call me Rolly. I hope *you* will, too. So, right after that

I took instruction. Oh, my poor head! It was so difficult. There was so much to memorize and I've a perfectly wretched memory, but I did it. I don't like to seem carping or to be finding fault with the Church but if they would only cut out all that memory work, things would be a lot *simpler* and they might pick up all sorts of really nice people, not that I'm implying they don't already have the best people. Good evening, Jimmy, Jack, Allen. Enjoying yourselves? But as I was saying, except for that awful memory work at the start, it's been thrilling. I go to confessional once a month and I even get to the Sunday-morning Mass, the one at ten, and *really* I think I'm something of a model convert.

"Of course it will probably be years before I die; I certainly *hope* it will be years. But when I go, I want to be prepared. I've picked out the nicest crypt at the Church of St. Agnes in Detroit. That's where my family makes those awful motorcars. And I shall be buried there. I expect the cardinal will officiate at the funeral. He better, considering the money I'm leaving them in my will. Going so soon, Rudy? Thank you, good night. I understand that the Pope is thinking quite seriously of giving me a decoration for the good deeds I've done. I've given them rather a bit of cash, you know. It's the only way to defeat Communism.

"I do hope I'll go to Heaven after doing so many good works on earth. I think sin is *terribly* fearsome, don't you? It's practically impossible not to sin a little, but I think it's the *big* sins that are the ones that can't be forgiven, like murdering people. A few lies, white lies, and an occasional infidelity, that's really the extent of my personal falls from Grace. I have such hopes for the afterlife. I see it as a riot of color! And all the angels will look like Marines. Too gay! The party is going well, don't you think?"

Jim agreed, weary of the flood of talk.

"If you'll excuse me I must make my rounds. The work of a hostess is never done. You wouldn't like to spend the night, would you?"

As Jim started to say no, Rolly giggled. "So few people do anymore, that's one of the horrors of age. Well, I've enjoyed this little chat with you *immensely,* and I hope you'll come by some evening when we can have a *quiet* dinner together." Rolloson patted Jim on the buttocks and plunged into his menagerie.

Jim found Shaw drunk and surrounded by sailors.

"I'm going home."

"But it's early. Come on, what you need is a drink."

"I'll call you up in a day or so." Jim departed. It was a relief for him to breathe the fresh air of the street.

Winter passed swiftly. Jim saw Shaw occasionally and Shaw was friendly and amusing and introduced him to a number of people who had money and nothing to do. There were many different homosexual worlds in New York, and each usually had some knowledge of the others. There was also the half-world where hetero- and homosexual mingled with a certain degree of frankness; this was particularly true of theatrical and literary groups. But in the highest society, the homosexual wore a stylized mask in order to move gracefully, and often convincingly, among admiring women who were attracted to him because his understanding was as great as his demands were few. Occasionally two homosexuals might meet in the great world. When they did, by a quick glance they acknowledged one another and, like amused conspirators, observed the effect each was having. It was a form of freemasonry.

From all over the country homosexuals had converged on New York. Here, among the indifferent millions, they could be as unnoticed by the enemy as they were known to one another. Yet for every one who lived openly with men, there were ten who married, had children, lived a discreet, ordinary life, only occasionally straying into bars or Turkish baths, particularly at five o'clock, that hour between office and home when the need for relief is particularly urgent. These masculine, rather tense men appealed to Jim, who disliked the other sort he met through Shaw. Yet he learned a great deal from the bold homosexuals. Like jazz musicians and dope addicts, they spoke in code. The words *fairy* and *pansy* were considered to be in bad taste. They preferred to say that a man was *gay*, while someone quite effeminate was a *queen*. As for those manly youths who offered themselves for seduction while proclaiming their heterosexuality, they were known as *trade*, since they usually wanted money. Trade was regarded with great suspicion; in fact, it was a part of the homosexual credo that this year's trade is next year's competition. Jim was thought to be trade by most of Shaw's friends, and inaccessible trade at that.

All during the winter Jim saw a good deal of the Rolloson world. Though he was repelled by the queens, he had no other society. Furtive encounters with young married men seldom led to anything. For a time, he hoped that if he saw enough of the queens, he might begin to like their society and be happy in it. But this was not possible, and so when Shaw went back on active duty, Jim dropped out of the gay world, preferring to haunt those bars where he could find young men like himself.

On an impulse one afternoon, Jim telephoned Maria Verlaine's hotel and to his surprise he found her in. She invited him to come to see her. Maria embraced him at the door. "You look so well!" She led him into the sitting room. Her eyes were luminous; she was vivacious; she laughed often. Then Jim noticed that her hands shook as she smoked her cigarette, and that she was ill at ease. He wondered why, but she gave him no clue. "Where have I been? Well, let me see. Everywhere. Nowhere. The summer in Maine. Then Jamaica. But New York is the center where I touch base between excursions."

"You haven't been happy, have you?" Jim was direct.

"What a question!" She laughed, eyes not meeting his. "It's hard to say *what* being happy is. Absence of pain? In that case, I have been happy. I suffer no pain. Feel nothing." But she mocked herself as she spoke.

"Then you still haven't got what you want?"

"No, I haven't. I live entirely on the surface, from day to day." She was suddenly grave.

"Will you ever find him?"

"I don't know. Perhaps not. I'm not young. I won't live forever. I simply go on. And wait."

"I wonder if any man wants the complete thing that you do. I don't think men are capable of so much feeling, that's why so many prefer one another to women." He was immediately sorry that he had said this. Yet he was convinced that it was the truth.

Maria laughed. "You don't leave us much hope, do you? One must be what one is. Besides, at times I have been very happy."

"Maybe we'd all be better off just having friends and forget about lovers."

Maria smiled. "That seems like such a waste, doesn't it?"

They talked then of other things until it was twilight and Jim got up to leave. Maria had told him that she was expecting a friend at five.

"I'll see you again. Soon," she said.

"Soon," said Jim. They did not embrace when he left.

Jim went straight to a Times Square bar frequented by soldiers and sailors. He studied the room carefully, like a general surveying the terrain of battle. Then he selected his objective: a tall Army lieutenant with broad shoulders, dark hair, blue eyes. Jim squeezed in beside him and ordered a drink. Jim's leg touched the lieutenant's leg, a hard muscular leg which returned the pressure.

"You in the service?" asked the lieutenant. His voice was slow, deep Far Western.

"Yeah, I was in the Army, too."

"What outfit?"

They exchanged information. The lieutenant had served with the infantry during the invasion of North Africa. He was now stationed in the South as an instructor.

"You live around here?"

Jim nodded. "I got a room downtown."

"I sure wish I had a place. I got to stay on a sofa with this married cousin."

"That sounds pretty uncomfortable."

"It sure is."

"You could," said Jim, as though he were thinking it over, "stay at my place. There's plenty of room."

The lieutenant said no, he couldn't do that; they had another drink together and then went home to bed.

II

IN THE SPRING, JIM returned to the courts. According to his partners, it might be ten years before the lot was built on; meanwhile, it was a gold mine and Jim worked hard, and he made money.

New York was full of servicemen, coming and going. Jim moved to a larger apartment, though still in the Village. He now knew a number of people but none well. It was easier to have sex with a man than to acquire a friend.

Jim saw Maria Verlaine once or twice, but, since it was obviously painful for her to be with him, he stopped telephoning her.

That summer Sullivan returned and Jim went to meet him at his club. They greeted each other in a gruff, offhand manner. Sullivan was thinner than Jim remembered and his sand-colored hair was beginning to go gray. He wore civilian clothes. "Yes, I'm through with being a correspondent." He grinned. "I quit before they fired me. I just don't have the vulgar touch, unlike my angel wife."

"Amelia?"

Sullivan nodded. "She's a great success. She started out by telling the *Ladies' Home Journal* what it was like to be a British housewife during the Blitz, and now she's graduated to the higher politics. Everyone quotes her. The Dark Ages continue." Sullivan ordered another drink for himself. "Have you seen Maria?"

"A few times. Not much. She's out of town."

"Too bad. I wanted to see her. You know she's almost the only woman I've ever really liked as a person. She's so un . . . pressing."

"I think she's all right now." Jim was tentative.

Sullivan waited.

"Interested in some man or other. I don't know who," Jim continued doggedly, not certain why he was lying except that he did not want to hurt Sullivan again.

"Well, that's nice for her. She deserves good luck." He changed the subject. "What about your business?"

Jim was proud to be able to tell him how well he was doing. Boasting to a friend is one of life's few certain pleasures.

"That's good news." Sullivan paused. "Are you alone; are you living alone?"

Jim nodded. "I just play the bars. I like strangers, I guess."

"It's better to have one person . . . isn't it?"

"Maybe for some people. But not for me," he lied. "Sometimes I never even know their names. Sometimes we never say more than a few words. It all happens so natural, so easy."

"Sounds lonely."

"Isn't everything?"

Sullivan sat back in his chair and looked about the old-fashioned bar with its dark heavy wood. Several club members sat drinking quietly at a corner table. "You've changed." Sullivan was casual.

"I know." Jim was as casual. "When you almost die, you change. When you've been a soldier, you change. When you get older, you change."

"You seem a little more . . . *definite,* now."

"About some things. But I still don't know how to get what I want."

Sullivan laughed. "Who does? Change is the nature of life."

"But that's not true," Jim continued, intent on his own thought.

"What?"

"There's someone I knew in Virginia. Someone I grew up with." It was the first time Jim had ever mentioned Bob to anyone. He stopped immediately.

"Who was he?"

"It was a long time ago." Jim said no more. But it gave him a sense of power to realize that he could one day recapture his past simply by going home. He made a vow. As soon as the work of the summer was done, he would go back to Virginia and find Bob, and complete what was begun that day by the river.

Jim was conscious that Sullivan had asked a question and was waiting for an answer. "What? I'm sorry."

"I said"—Sullivan was awkward—"that I was alone, too, and if you wanted to, we might . . . again."

Jim was flattered but not greatly moved. He responded amiably. Their affair was resumed. And since it was no longer of much importance to either of them, their life together was rather more pleasant than it had been the first time around.

In June, Paul's new novel was published and his publishers gave a cocktail party for him. The day was hot. Jim was bored and ill at ease, but Sullivan, immaculate in a new gabardine suit, was almost happy.

In the stifling room, the talk was loud as the flower of New York publishing got drunk together. Jim drifted from group to group, eyes smarting from cigarette smoke, puzzled by what conversation he did hear. "Henry James revival? It won't last. It's the British, you know. They're responsible. During air raids, people need to be comforted, so they read James and Trollope. Return to a safe golden self-contained world, with no bombs in it."

"I suppose there will be war novels. The real horror of war is the novels which are written about it. But don't expect anything good for at least a decade. I wouldn't publish a war book for the world. Harry Brown of course is an exception. John Hersey, too."

"Carson McCullers? Yes. And of course Faulkner. The Agrarians, yes. A lot of Southerners seem to be writing. Perhaps it was the Civil War. One must have a tragedy to have a literature. Also, Southerners are not forced so quickly into business. That makes a difference. And then they talk so awfully much."

"Is the *Partisan Review* really, truly Trotskyite?"

"The Jews can't write novels. No, I'm not anti-Semitic.

And Jews do make excellent critics. But they are not creative. It has something to do with Talmudic training. Of course Proust was a genius but he was half-French and all social climber."

"Henry Miller is almost as boring as Walt Whitman, and a good deal less talented."

"I adored *For Whom the Bell Tolls*. I read it twice. Obscenity of an obscenity but it was beautiful and good and true."

"Scott Fitzgerald? I don't think I know the name. Is he here? Does he write?"

A lean young man in need of a shave asked Jim if he was a writer and when Jim said no, the young man was relieved. "Too many writers," he mumbled. He was drunk.

"What do you think of Paul Sullivan?" Jim was curious to know. But he found the answer unfathomable. "I don't like Aldous Huxley either."

Across the room Sullivan was signing a book. Jim departed.

It was a busy summer. The war continued. Jim's work was hard but rewarding. He particularly liked Mr. Globe, who knew nothing about tennis. "I'm in this for the money, Jim," he said one day. "I used to have this secondhand shop and that closed in the Depression. And then I was a clerk until I got into this for the money. I say you can make money easy if you're in things for the money but you need a little help sometimes. You know why we let you buy in the business?"

Jim shook his head, though he knew.

"Because you're not in this just for the money. You like what you do and there's always got to be a few people who know something to help the ones who're in it for the money to make money."

That summer they made money, and Jim was happy.

When Maria Verlaine returned to New York that autumn, Jim and Sullivan visited her at the Harding. She was in good form, Jim thought, and told her so.

"I've been in Argentina."

"Is that an answer?" Sullivan laughed.

"I thought you were in Canada," said Jim.

"Yes, to both of you. I'll get you a drink. I thought we'd have dinner here in the room." Her movements were swift and graceful. "It's a very simple, a very familiar story. I met an Argentine in Canada. He invited me to visit him in Buenos Aires. I did."

"Was that wise?" Paul was oddly conventional.

"Dear Paul! He's a rich poet and quite indifferent to what people say. As a matter of fact, he told everyone I was a famous literary figure from Mexico and I was worshiped. It was delightful."

"And now?"

"I'm back, as you see, and we'll be here for the winter."

"We?" asked Jim.

"Yes, Carlos is here with me. But in a different suite. We must be hypocrites in New York. We don't want to corrupt the Anglo-Saxons."

"Is he published in America?" asked Paul.

She shook her head. "I don't think he's ever really written anything."

"But you said he was a poet."

"That doesn't mean he has to write poems, does it? Actually, he does nothing at all and that's his poetry, to do nothing, with imagination of course."

"Are we going to meet him?" asked Paul.

Maria was evasive. "Of course. But not today. Perhaps later. Now tell me about your new book."

Jim listened and wondered why he felt betrayed instead

of pleased for Maria, who seemed to have found what she had been searching for. But he was not pleased. He was furious with her and with himself for being unable to give her anything except a friendship and a candor she could get as easily from others quite as understanding as he. Yet he was hurt; it was as if she had indeed been a lover who had deserted him.

Dinner was brought them in the room, and Jim drank prewar Burgundy, hoping to get drunk, but his mind was too sharply focused in its outrage.

During dinner Paul described his London meeting with Amelia. Maria was not surprised. "I was afraid she would become an Amazon."

"Now don't blame it on me."

"Never! It was not your fault, not hers. It's just this terrible country."

"Terrible?" Jim was startled from his self-pity. He had never heard anyone be quite so vehement about God's country.

"Maria's a Nazi." Paul chuckled. "Or a Communist."

"The Russians are our allies." Maria was light. "But I'm not political. Just a woman. A rather hard thing to be in your country. Either I meet men who have been . . . wounded, or I meet those who think only of women as a kind of relief, rather like aspirin."

"Latents are lousy lovers." Paul grinned. He had never been impressed by Maria's hymns to Aphrodite.

"You are perfectly right." Maria chose to take him seriously. "Everything in this country is calculated to destroy both sexes. Men are told that their desires are dirty and unwanted. Women are told that they are goddesses and that men are fortunate to be able just to worship them at a distance. . . ."

"It's the fault of advertising," said Paul. "Since women buy the most things, the advertisers flatter them the most, tell them they have more taste than men, more sensitivity, more intelligence, even more physical strength because they live longer. The advertisers of course are men."

"Well, they have a lot to answer for." Maria was uncharacteristically grim.

"Are Europeans so much better?" asked Jim.

Maria shrugged. "At least the men know who and what they are, and that is the beginning of sanity."

Paul agreed. "Americans tend to play different roles, hoping that somehow they'll stumble on the right one."

Jim turned to Maria. "When the war is over, will you go back to Europe?"

"Yes. Forever!"

"With the Argentine?" Paul was amused.

"Who knows?" She smiled. She had never seemed quite so lovely to Jim. "I live in the present." She looked at Jim and because he saw affection in her eyes, he looked away, pondering the betrayal, cursing its cause.

III

SULLIVAN'S NEW BOOK WAS not a success. He wrote articles for magazines and wondered if he should try his luck in the theater. Jim found him easy to get along with. From time to time one or the other would bring home a stranger and neither was in the least jealous or envious. From Jim's standpoint it was an ideal relationship; only the intense experience with Bob could be more satisfactory than his life with Sullivan.

Jim saw Maria Verlaine occasionally; the Argentine was

never present. Their old intimacy continued, but he was aware, now more than ever, that it was not enough. He found it unbearable that she should be happy and that he was not the cause.

At New Year's Rolloson invited Jim and Sullivan to a party: "a congenial group, my dears, just a little gathering" of what turned out to be the same group that had been there at the time of Jim's first visit. Rolloson wore a light gray suit pulled in tightly at the waist, a mauve shirt gorgeously monogrammed, and a sea green crepe de chine ascot at his rosy throat. He greeted them at the door, smelling of violets.

"How lovely of you to come, Mr. Sullivan. May I call you Paul? Paul, there are loads of people here *dying* to meet you and I'm sure you'll find a lot of old friends, too. I think literally *everybody* is here, and I did so intend to have an *intimate* party. Ah, well." He thrust Sullivan at a group of literary-looking men, among whom was the gray-haired professor from City College. With Sullivan safely put aside, Rolly took Jim about the room, introducing him to various people, all the while chattering. "First Shaw and now Sullivan. Aren't you the one, though! How do you do it? Or should I say, *what* do you have?" He gave Jim a lightning grope. Jim shied away, irritated.

"It just happens that they're the only people I know."

"But *where* did you know them?"

"In Hollywood. Did you get your Papal thing, that decoration?"

Rolly frowned. "My dear, the Church is riddled with politics, literally riddled. As a matter of fact—don't repeat a word of this to *anyone*—I think I shall take up Vedanta. I've met the most wonderful swami. At least I think he's a swami. He's here tonight unless I forgot . . . no, I remember I saw him at the Van Vechtens' and I invited him . . . or was that the prince? I've got the most wonderful Hindu prince here, too. You'll just love him. He looks like Theda Bara. *He's* here, I know, because I remember compliment-ing him on his handsome turban. But I'm not so sure about the swami. You know, he's got millions of dollars in rubies and emeralds right here with him in New York—the prince, I mean, not the swami. I don't think *he* has anything but he's terribly high-*minded*. Read Gerald Heard if you don't believe me. Where's Shaw now?"

"Who? Oh, Shaw. Well, I think he's back in Hollywood by now. He's been discharged from the Navy, or so it said in the papers."

"Papers? Don't you ever hear from him?"

"No, we don't write."

"What a pity! You know, he broke so many hearts when he was here. Good evening Jack, Jimmy, Allen. Lovely of you to come. I think he's terribly handsome—Shaw, I mean. He has such an *air* about him." Rolly looked about the room at his guests. Jim noticed that he was wearing makeup. "It's very gay, don't you think so? Oh, here comes Sir Roger Beaston, the perfect *camp*! Do excuse me." Rolly darted across the room to meet a pale little man with yellow hair.

Jim found Sullivan at the center of a group of people, not all literary. They were drinking champagne and talking animatedly about a certain European king who had taken a new boy who was supposed to be extraordinarily handsome and charming, even if he *had* begun his career hustling in Miami. Jim listened, no longer surprised at hearing revela-tions about people he had never suspected before. At first he had disbelieved all the stories on principle, but too often they had proved to be true. Obviously the world was not what it seemed. Anything might be true of anybody.

Jim ambled away. In the hall he found a telephone, cradled in a piece of driftwood. Without thinking he picked it up and telephoned Maria. She answered. He could hear music behind her voice and the sound of voices.

"Jim! Where are you?"

"At a dull party."

"Then come here!"

Maria wore an evening dress of silver and a red flower in her hair. Her eyes sparkled and she seemed drunk, although she never drank. She simply became charged with energy and enthusiasm when she was with those she liked. They embraced and she led him into her apartment. Maria introduced him to a dozen handsome couples, mostly European émigrés. Then she gave him champagne and they sat in front of the mock fireplace.

"Whose party did you desert for me?"

"A man named Rolloson."

She made a face. "I've known Rolly for twenty years. He's harmless, I suppose, but he alarms me. It's like seeing oneself in a distorted mirror."

"We only went . . . well, because we were asked to come." He felt awkward because she had not invited him originally to her party. Sensing this, she said, "You know why I didn't ask you?"

"Carlos?"

She nodded.

"Is he here now, in this room?"

"No, he's gone downstairs to order more champagne. It won't hurt you to see him, to meet him?"

"No, of course not. I'd like to."

Then the bells began to ring and over the radio came the noise from Times Square and everyone exclaimed, "Happy

New Year!" and Carlos returned and kissed Maria. "I was almost too late," he said. She turned to Jim. "This is Carlos, Jim."

They shook hands. "Happy New Year," said Carlos.

"Happy New Year," said Jim. In a few minutes he went home.

CHAPTER
10

I

IN THE SPRING SULLIVAN received an advance from a publisher to write a book about Africa. "And that means six months of traveling, all expenses paid. If I don't take it, you'll have to support me."

"Not if I can help it." Jim was guiltily pleased at the thought of living alone again.

"Funny thing about travel, once you start, it's hard to stop. Like being an alcoholic. I really want to go."

"So do I. But I've got work to do."

"And someone else to find." This was flat.

"I'm not exactly looking." Jim was sharp.

"I know." Contrition. "I'm sorry. Anyway, there is something wrong with two men living together, a man and a woman, too, for that matter. Unless they have children, it's pointless."

"We're too selfish, I suppose."

"And separate. Perhaps a good thing. I don't agree with Maria's high romantic view of love. We affect one another quite enough merely by existing. Whenever the stars cross, or is it comets? fragments pass briefly from one orbit to another. On rare occasions there is total collision, but most often the two simply continue without incident, neither losing more than a particle to the other, in passing."

So they separated, with a metaphor involving stars.

The next day, as if by further celestial design, there was a letter from Mrs. Willard, full of news.

"You remember Bob Ford, don't you?" she wrote. "He was such a friend of yours in school. Well, he's in the Merchant Marine now and he was home on leave for a few days last week. He asked after you and so did his wife. I don't know if I ever wrote you that he married Sally Mergendahl last year, and they have a baby. You know that job with the school is still open and if you want to come back . . ."

There it was. Bob had returned. But he was married. Not once had it occurred to Jim that Bob could ever in any way be different from the way he had been that day beside the river. Yet he must have changed. He had married Sally. Jim experienced a sudden panic. Was it possible that he had waited years for a reunion with a man who cared only for women? No. He rejected the thought. Bob was obviously bisexual, if only because no one could have been so perfect a lover on that unique occasion and then change entirely. Jim reassured himself, and because he wanted to believe that nothing had changed, nothing changed, in his mind. Meanwhile, he made plans to go back to Virginia as soon as summer ended and take up his life at the precise point where it had left off that green summer evening seven years before.

. . .

During the summer Shaw came to town for the premiere of someone else's picture and Jim met him in a restaurant where the food and service were bad but where many people who were famous came to look not only at one another but also at themselves in the mirrors which lined the dining room.

Jim was startled to find that Shaw was gray at the temples; he was moving with unusual dispatch into middle age.

"You're looking handsome, Jimmy," said Shaw, "really handsome, I must say. Of all my graduates, you're easily the best-looking."

"That's like winning the Davis Cup. Thanks." Jim smiled. "Who're you living with now?"

"Nobody. I was with a perfect son of a bitch, from Detroit, a diver, of all things—you know, Olympic Games stuff. He had a wonderful build but stupid! My God, I don't think I've ever known anybody so stupid. All he wanted to do was drink beer and sit up late in gay bars. I kicked him out. Anyway, he had a wife and two children so I really think I did the right thing, don't you? Nobody wants to break up a home. What have you been doing?"

"Working."

"Sullivan?"

"Gone to Africa."

"Hope they eat him." Shaw was sour. "He's such a pretentious bastard. I saw where his new book got bad notices. Not that critics mean a thing. When they pan my pictures I make money, and when they praise them we lose it. After all, entertainment is entertainment."

Jim noticed that everyone in the room was aware of Shaw, but for once Jim disliked the attention; particularly when he noticed several men he had met at Rolloson's party: each accompanied by a woman, for this was enemy territory.

"Are you making a picture?"

"No. It's hard to get the right roles nowadays. I'm sitting it out. The studio thinks the war is going to be over and they'll get the old stars back and to hell with us who've been selling the tickets for them. Well, they'll find out. Gable means nothing now."

Jim wondered if Shaw was finished. It was a harsh business, as everyone liked to say.

"They'll come back to me in time. But it'll be too late."

"Why?"

Shaw looked about him; then he whispered, "I'm quitting the movies, retiring."

"And do nothing?"

"Not quite. I'm going on the stage. I start rehearsing in September."

"That's wonderful."

"But tough. I've never been on a stage, but I've got to do it."

"How's your mother?"

"Still in Baltimore. It's a funny thing, she brags about me, of course, but sometimes I think she resents my success. Imagine a mother being competitive! I guess people are people, first. Anyway, she's happy about me being married."

"Married?"

Shaw nodded. "It's the studio's idea. They think too many people are catching on. Maybe they're right."

"Who's the girl?"

"Calla Petra. Hungarian actress. Kept by the head of the studio, lost a hundred thousand dollars one night gambling at Vegas. A real tramp. But I won't give her a penny. He'll have to. We've signed a prenuptial agreement, ironclad. No money from me. She's a dyke, anyway, and she needs the publicity as much as I do."

"Sounds real cozy."

"Sounds awful." Shaw groaned.

They saw each other often during the summer. The day Shaw's play opened, he announced that he was retiring from the screen; a week later the play closed, and Shaw went back to Hollywood. His wedding to Calla Petra was the most glittering of the season.

After Shaw left New York, Jim returned to the bar life. He particularly liked one Eighth Avenue bar where both men and women gathered and some of the men were available and some were not, which gave a certain excitement to negotiations. He most liked the innocents who would say the next morning, "Gee, I was sure drunk last night!" and pretend not to remember what had happened.

One heavy summer night, Jim stood at the bar nursing a beer, examining the inmates. He had almost settled on a young Marine with blue eyes and buck teeth when a voice behind him said, "Ain't you Willard?"

Jim looked around and saw a fat bald young sailor. "That's right, and you're . . . ?" He couldn't recall.

"Collins, Alaska. Remember?"

"Sure. Come on. Have a drink."

Collins squeezed in beside him at the bar. "I'm Navy now. I was a petty officer but I got busted."

"What happened?"

"I got pissed and told a commander off. My usual trouble. Were you in the service?"

"Army. I been out a year."

"What're you doing now?"

Jim told him.

"Coining money."

"Fair. You in town long?"

"No, we're sailing soon. This is my last liberty. Boy, you got a good deal, living here, with your own business. I wish I was in your shoes."

"What're you going to do when you get out?"

"Me? I'm a sailor. What else? I don't know anything else. Once I tried to work in this machine shop, but I couldn't stand being in one place so long, so I quit, left my wife, went back to sea."

"You're married?"

"Divorced. I knew her since I was a kid in school and she always wanted to marry me but I wouldn't until I got drunk one night and knocked her up and she said I'd *have* to marry her and so I did. We got a kid who lives with her, that's in Eugene, Oregon."

"Too bad." Jim tried to sound sympathetic.

"I guess some guys just aren't meant to be family men and I'm one of them. I got this chick in Seattle now who's panting to be married but I told her, I been stung once and I'm not going to get stung again. You married yet?"

"No," said Jim. "Not yet."

"You're smarter than me. But I'll bet you got a girl in New York?"

"Kind of." Jim was noncommittal.

Collins took a long swallow of his drink and said, "You know any girls around town?"

Jim shook his head. "Just one. You see, I've been working pretty hard and . . ."

"I know how it is. Say, where did you go after you skipped ship?"

"L.A."

"Man, that's *my* town! Wide open. Where all the chicks

want a good time, like us, and no talk about marrying or any of that shit. You ever see any movie stars?"

"Some."

"Like who?"

"Calla Petra."

"No kidding! She must be something the way she's stacked. You get to talk to her?"

"Oh, lots of times."

"No kidding! You bang her?"

"No, I just played tennis with her."

"I'd sure like to play tennis with her." Collins leered. "And that ain't all I'd like to play with her."

Jim ordered another beer. Usually he could keep the same beer going for an hour, but Collins made him nervous and he found himself actually drinking the beer, an unusual gesture.

"You like the Navy?"

Collins shrugged. "They don't know nothing about the sea, that's for sure. Wished I was back in the Merchant Marine."

"Why aren't you?"

"I was on land with my wife and I was going to be drafted. So to get out of the draft, I joined the Navy, because I didn't want to be in no Army where I had to walk."

As they drank together, Jim looked about the bar. The Marine had gone. There was no one else who appealed to him. At the opposite end of the bar an old man was trying to make a sailor who in turn was trying to make a soldier. It was very funny. Collins, perfectly unaware of the comedy, suddenly asked, "Hey, why did you leave the ship in such a hurry?"

It was a question Jim had been waiting for. He spoke slowly, simulating ease. "I wanted to see California and I

didn't want to have to argue with the steward, so I just
skipped out."

"I figured it was something like that." Collins finished his
drink. "How come you left those girls in that apartment?
That was one thing I never been able to figure out."

Jim shrugged. "I didn't like the one I had, that's all."

"Well, she was madder than hell, but you was smart to
leave when you did."

"Why?"

"They both had clap. And I caught it and had a hell of a
time getting cured." They both laughed and Collins told
Jim about the man who had had clap twenty times and been
cured every time except the first. At last they parted and Jim
was relieved that Collins's liberty was almost over and they
would not meet again.

II

ONE COLD DAY WHEN the winter sky was bitter orange and
gray and a chill haze hung over the city, Jim went home for
Christmas.

Mrs. Willard stood on the porch as her son came up the
path to the house. He was startled at her appearance. White
hair, untidy as always, face pale and lined; she had grown
old while he was away. They embraced and she clung to
him, holding him tight, saying nothing, only holding him.
Then they went into the house, where, at least, nothing had
changed. The parlor was as depressing as ever, despite a
Christmas tree, glittering with small buzzing lights. Jim felt
oddly displaced in time. He turned to his mother and they
looked at one another without speaking, two strangers with
a common memory.

"You've grown up, Jim," his mother said at last. "You've changed."

"We all do, I guess." He was inadequate.

"You look more like my side of the family. You don't look like your father anymore. You used to."

Jim saw in his mother's face his own features grown old and he was frightened at the thought of age and death.

"You haven't changed much," he lied.

She chuckled. "Oh, yes, I have. I'm an old woman now. But I don't mind. If you haven't got beauty in the first place, age makes you better-looking, they say, gives you character."

He looked at her face in the light of the Christmas tree and he agreed with her. She had improved with time. She had achieved a face of her own, something she had lacked before.

"Are you going to get married, son?" It was strange to be called *son* again.

"Someday."

"The older I get the more I think people should be married early. I sometimes think that the reason your father and I never got along as well as we should was because we married so late. You're just the right age to settle down."

"Perhaps."

"There're some nice girls growing up here. They'd make fine wives. You'll meet them while you're home. You should marry a nice girl here rather than one of those New York girls, not that it's any of my business." Jim smiled: New York people were not very well thought of in the South.

She asked him about his work and he told her about it. She was pleased. "I'm glad you're making money. Nobody in this family ever has before and it's about time somebody did. But money's not everything, is it? I mean sometimes marriage and settling down and enjoying life are more important, don't you think so?" Sooner or later she would suggest that he stay home for good.

"I don't know, Mother. I really haven't thought much about settling down yet. I've got a good business in New York and as long as it's good I better stay with it."

Sensing resistance, she changed the subject. "Your brother is a second lieutenant now. He's in the Air Force and he's going overseas any day. Why, I don't know, since the war's almost over, or so the papers say."

"Will he be here for Christmas?"

She nodded. "He's got a few days' leave. He's a very bright young man." Jim wondered if perhaps she disliked her younger son. His mother was definitely changed. Anything was possible.

"You're taking in boarders now?"

She had written him this news. "Just a couple, a man and wife. You'll meet them at dinner. Carrie and her husband are coming to dinner, too."

"How's my nephew?"

"Nice and fat." She paused. "I can't get over how you've changed," she said finally. They were silent. Jim idly kicked his suitcase and his mother said, "You'd better take your things up to your room."

"Which one?"

"Your old room."

"Does John stay there when he's on leave?"

"Yes. Nothing's changed. I try not to change anything if I can help it. I know that's maybe living too much in the past but I think the past was pretty nice, in some ways. I think maybe the future can be even nicer."

"You mean since Father died." Jim was blunt.

She nodded placidly. "Yes, since your father died. I always

believed if you make a bad bargain, you just have to keep it. But when it's over, there's no use pretending that it was the best thing that ever happened."

"Why did you marry him?"

"Lord, son, why does anyone marry anybody? If I ever knew why I married him, I've forgotten. Probably because he asked me. I wasn't in much demand. Now take your bag up and get ready for dinner."

Everyone was at table when Jim came into the dining room. His mother introduced him to the boarders; then he shook hands with his brother-in-law and kissed his sister. Carrie had grown stout. Her breasts and hips seemed ready to burst her clothes. Without makeup, she looked tired but good-humored, and obviously she was pleased with her husband, an amiable sort who did whatever she asked him to.

"Well, Mother, he's as beautiful as ever." Carrie looked at her brother admiringly. "He sure got all the looks in this family." Her laugh was like an explosion and only stopped when her husband told her what she wanted to hear: that she was beautiful, too.

During dinner, they spoke of Jim's work and whether or not it was profitable, and if he came home, as they all desired, could he do as well as he had done in New York? And of course Carrie asked the inevitable: "When are you going to get married, Jim?"

He shrugged. "When some girl asks me." Everyone laughed at that.

"You were always shy with the girls," said his sister, her mouth full. "You really ought to settle down. There's nothing like it, is there, dear?" Her husband agreed that there was nothing like it. Jim found the masquerade depressing. He tried to change the subject and failed.

"Jim will marry when he's ready to settle down," said his

mother tranquilly. "I think he's been wise not to have gotten married while he was traipsing around the world."

They talked of marriage, secure people whose lives followed a familiar pattern, the experience of one very much like that of the other. But when they tried to advise Jim, none suspected that their collective wisdom was of no use to him, that the pattern of his life was different from theirs. This fact made him sad, as well as annoyed at the never-ending masquerade. He was bored by his own necessary lies. How he longed to tell them exactly what he was! He wondered suddenly what would happen if every man like himself were to be natural and honest. Life would certainly be better for everyone in a world where sex was thought of as something natural and not fearsome, and men could love men naturally, in the way they were meant to, as well as to love women naturally, in the way they were meant to. But even as he sat at the table, pondering freedom, he knew that it was a dangerous thing to be an honest man; finally, he lacked the courage.

"By the way," said Carrie, "you knew Bob Ford married Sally Mergendahl, didn't you?"

"Mother wrote me. Where is he . . . where are they now?"

"She's living here with her family, and he's at sea, but I think he's due back in a few days. He'll be here for the Christmas party the Mergendahls are giving. You're invited. And they have the cutest baby girl, with dark red hair just like Bob's."

"Why, Jim, I would never have recognized you, so grown up and everything! Isn't he, dear?" Mrs. Mergendahl turned to Mr. Mergendahl and got his agreement. She continued, secure in her audience. "Well, he's a grown man now. They all are. Seems like only yesterday when you played in all those tennis tournaments at school. Now look at you! And all the other boys in the Army, married, and our own little girl a mother!"

Mr. Mergendahl winked at Jim. "You better let him go, Mother, so he can meet the young girls who are dying to meet him. Got a whole new crop of 'em, too." Jim excused himself and went into the crowded, old-fashioned living room. Carrie took him by the arm. "I'll introduce you around."

Many of the people he recognized; some he had known in school, others from the town. Everyone remembered him and they seemed genuinely glad he was back, recalling events that he had forgotten. As in a dream, he moved from group to group, toward a central point where he knew Bob must be.

Then he saw Sally Mergendahl—now Sally Ford—and he broke away from Carrie to talk to her. Sally was now a tall graceful woman with dark hair braided about her head. They shook hands warmly, each scrutinizing the other, looking for signs of change.

"Congratulations!" said Jim.

"On the baby? Or marrying Bob?"

"Both." Jim sounded blithe; yet she was his rival.

"That's sweet of you, Jim. Here, let's sit down. There's so much we have to catch up on." They sat on a horsehair sofa, their conversation broken regularly by newcomers who wanted to say hello to Jim.

"See how popular you are? Oh, you really ought to settle down here with the rest of us."

"You heard I wasn't going to?"

"Well, not exactly, but you know how everybody knows everybody else's business around here. We spend all our time prying, even though there's never anything very interesting going on. We all know each other too well."

"Where's Bob?"

She frowned. "Newport News, with his ship. He won't be in until tomorrow. When he does get here, why don't you have dinner with us, just the three of us?"

"I'd like to. Bob's a first mate now, isn't he?"

"Yes. But he's quitting when the war's over."

"How come? He loves the sea."

"But Daddy needs him in the insurance business, and everybody thinks Bob will make a wonderful salesman, and Daddy says that when he retires Bob can have the company."

"That'll be nice for him." Jim saw the kindly noose being dropped over Bob's unwilling shoulders. But were they unwilling? Could he have changed? It was possible.

"He's roamed around long enough. After all, there's just so much world to see and then where are you? Anyway, all his friends are here and he can have a good job. I think everything will be just grand for us. I can't wait for you to see the baby."

"Is Bob a good . . . father?"

"Well, he hasn't had much practice. At the moment he thinks a baby is something to play with until it starts to cry, when he wants to wring its neck. Then he says that I care more about the baby than I do about him, so I tell him that, after all, the baby *is* him, which it is."

"Does he understand that?"

"Well . . . yes, at times. You know how he is."

"I don't know if I do anymore."

"It *has* been a long time, hasn't it? And he is different. Of course he looks about the same. But he laughs a lot more than he used to. He was rather grim when he was a boy. And of course he was girl crazy then. He still gets letters from girls all over the world. He lets me read them and they're really pathetic. But I'm not jealous. I don't know why. I guess it's because he came back to me, when he didn't have to."

As she talked, Jim wondered if Bob had ever been attracted to men. From what she said—and what he suspected—it seemed unlikely, which meant that their experience had been unique. And that meant Bob had made love with him not out of a lust for the male but from affection. The fact that he now preferred women to men could only make their relationship all the more unusual and binding.

Jim did not deceive himself that his return would mean an end to Bob's marriage. Their boyhood dream of going to sea together was no longer practical. Too much had happened. Each was now part of the world. Yet there was no reason why the affair could not continue, particularly if he returned to Virginia and took the job at the high school. Proximity would do the rest. He wondered about the old slave cabin by the river. Was it still there?

Sally was still talking. "I don't like to be old-fashioned. And I really don't think I am. I believe a man should have lots of affairs with women before he settles down with one. I told my mother that and I thought she would explode. She says she never *will* be able to understand the younger generation."

"When do you think Bob will be out of the Merchant Marine?"

"When the war with Germany's over. So they say. Daddy has a friend in Washington who can fix it if there's any problem. Jim, would you get me some punch? I'm parched."

Jim crossed the crowded living room, smiling at all the people who wanted to talk to him. He was surprised that he was popular. If only they knew. At the punch bowl he found himself face to face with his brother.

John was tall and dark and he looked trim in his uniform. Jim disliked him as much as ever. He was astonishingly self-confident and everyone said that he was going "to make his mark" and he believed it, too. Politics was to be his career.

"What's up, Jim? It's been a long time." John's voice was rich and deep; he had been drinking too much, Jim noticed. They exchanged greetings and perfunctory compliments. Then John indicated Sally. "She's very nice, isn't she?"

"Yes. I like her."

"Shame Bob missed the party. You must be looking forward to seeing him again."

Jim wondered if John knew about him. His brother was shrewd and he obviously remembered how much Jim had seen of Bob when they were boys. But was that enough to make him suspicious? Or did it take one to know one? Jim smiled to himself at the thought. It often ran in families, they said. He gave his brother a speculative look.

"What's the matter?"

"Oh . . . nothing. I was just thinking. Well, I better get Sally her punch."

"Don't get caught under any mistletoe," said John in his deep mocking voice.

"What took you so long?" Sally was pleasant. "I was afraid you'd deserted me."

"No, I was just talking to my brother."

"It must be wonderful to be back," said Sally Ford.

The day of the dinner came and Jim was nervous. He snapped at his mother when she told him that he should wear an overcoat, and he lost his temper with his brother, whose fountain pen in a bureau drawer had leaked all over his last white shirt. After a satisfactory row with John, Jim left the house.

With pounding heart, Jim knocked on the door of the Mergendahl house. Bob opened it.

In a daze, Jim shook hands, hardly able to speak.

"How the hell are you?" Bob was saying. "Come on in and have a drink." He led Jim into the living room. "The old folks are out for dinner and Sally's upstairs doing something or other to the baby. Gosh, but it's good to see you. You look the same. How've you been?"

Jim's voice was hoarse when he finally spoke. "Fine. I've been just fine. You look good, too." And Bob did.

Jim was surprised that he had forgotten what Bob looked like. He had always thought his mental picture of him as accurate, but apparently his memory was emotional, not literal. He had forgotten how dark Bob's red hair was, and that he had freckles and that his mouth curved up at the corners and that his eyes were as blue as the Arctic Sea. Only the body was as he recalled it, long and slim and heavy in the chest. He looked good in uniform.

They sat in front of the fireplace and Bob forgot to get the drinks. He too was taking inventory. Did he remember everything?

"You just disappeared," said Bob at last.

"Me? You! I wrote you and wrote you but you were never where I sent the letters."

"Well, I was on the move a lot, like you."

"We both were."

"Hey, you met Sally yet? Since you been back?"

"At the Christmas party."

"That's right. I forgot. She invited you for tonight."

"She's a wonderful girl." Jim wanted to establish that at the beginning.

"I'll say! I'm glad you like each other. You didn't really know her back at school, did you?"

"No. But I remember you used to go around with her even then."

"So when are *you* getting married?" That question again.

"Not for a while."

"You think you might come back here to live?"

Jim nodded. "I think I might. You'll be living here, won't you?"

"So they tell me. It looks like I'm going into the insurance business, with Sally's father. Everybody thinks I'll be good at it."

"But you'd rather be at sea?"

Bob moved uneasily in his chair, crossing and uncrossing his long legs. "Well, I've been at sea almost ten years now and I've made a place for myself. It won't be easy changing to land. But if Sally wants it . . ."

"She wants it. But you don't?"

"Yes, I do." Bob was defiant, even petulant. Then he shifted. "Well, maybe not."

"I don't see what's wrong with being a sailor, especially since you're making good money. Why wouldn't Sally like that?"

"You know women. They want you where they can look at you all the time. She says she doesn't feel she's married when I'm gone."

"So you'll settle here."

Bob nodded gloomily. "I'll settle here. Oh, I'll get used to it, all right. And I like the idea of being a family man."

"So I guess I'll be moving back, maybe."

"That'd be swell, just like it used to be. Funny, I knew all kinds of girls here but I never did know any of the guys very well, except you. It'd be nice having at least one buddy in town. To play tennis with."

"Yes."

"But you're too good for me. You're a pro and I haven't

played for years. But it sure would be nice to play again."
He was nostalgic and Jim felt an instant of triumph. Bob
would return to him, as easily, as naturally as he had gone
with him the first time.

"We had some good times when we were kids," said Bob
dreamily, looking into the fire. Jim looked, too. Yes, this
was the way it had been: fire and the mood of firelight. It
was going to happen again. He was certain of that.

"We had a good time." Jim vowed he would not mention
the cabin first.

"I wish sometimes that we had gone to the university
together. The sea was probably a mistake, though fun. You
only went because I did, didn't you?"

"That was one of the reasons."

"Do you think I . . . we made a mistake?"

Jim studied the fire. "No," he said finally. "We did what
we were meant to do. I think it was natural for you to be a
sailor and me to be a tennis player. We were never like the
other people around here. We weren't housebroken. We
got away. They hate that. Only now we're coming back."

Bob smiled. "You're the only person who understands
why I had to go to sea. Yes, we did do the right thing. But
now is it right to come back? *Can* you come back to living
in the same house, with the same people day after day? Is it
possible?"

"I don't know. I just don't know. Of course it's easier for
me. I can teach tennis here but you certainly can't be a
seaman on land. I guess you ought to do what you feel you
have to do." Jim spoke with something else in mind.

Bob sighed. "I can't make up my mind."

Jim wanted to help but he could not. "Wait," he said.
"Wait until something happens. Something always does."

They were silent before the fire. Jim could hear the
muffled sound of a baby crying upstairs, Bob's baby.

"How's your father?" asked Jim finally.

"Dead. Last month."

"Did you see him before he died?"

"No."

"Didn't he want to see you?"

"He was crazy, they say. He'd been crazy for the last five years. It wouldn't have done any good. Besides, I didn't want to see him. I didn't care if he died or not." Bob was matter of fact, all bitterness gone. "You got a girl, Jim?" he asked suddenly.

"No."

"That sounds like you. Still shy with women. But you ought to find yourself one. Changing around wears a guy out."

"Maybe I'll find somebody when I come back here."

"And then we'll be two married men. Gosh, we never thought of ourselves being that old, did we?"

"No, never."

"And in a few years we'll be middle-aged and then old and then dead."

"Morbid, isn't it?" They both laughed. Then Sally came into the room.

"Hello, Jim."

"How's the baby?" asked Bob.

"Asleep. Thank God! Bob! you haven't given Jim a drink."

"Sorry. What do you want?"

"Nothing, thanks."

"Then we'll go in to dinner," said Sally.

The dinner was good and they talked of the townspeople and their families and about the war in Germany. In the intimacy of the family dining room, Jim was completely at peace. He would not have to make a move. The thing was happening of its own accord. Soon Bob would be with him.

And, sure enough, it was Bob who maneuvered their lives into conjunction. "I think I'll be up in New York during May. Let's get together then and have one last fling before the old prison doors shut!"

Sally smiled indulgently.

Jim said, "That'd be wonderful. I'll give you my address and you call me as soon as you get to town."

III

THAT SPRING JIM TRIED to exhaust himself in work so that he would not think of Bob. But it was difficult. Nor did matters improve when May came and went and there was no word from Bob. Finally he wrote Sally, who told him that Bob was still at sea and wasn't it just awful? But at least the war was finally over and the Merchant Marine could not keep him much longer.

A year late Bob appeared at Jim's apartment. They shook hands as though they had seen each other only the day before.

"Swell place you got." Bob looked approvingly at the apartment. "Won't you hate to give this up for Virginia?"

"I haven't given it up yet." Jim smiled.

Bob sat in a chair and stretched his long legs. He still wore a uniform. "Swell place," he murmured again.

"When are you getting out?"

Bob frowned. "Damned if I know. I have a chance now to get master's papers. That's something at my age, and I hate turning it down."

"But Sally?"

"That's just it . . . but Sally. I don't know what I'm going to do. She wants me home."

"And you don't want to go?"

"No."

"Well, don't. It's your life. If you're happy at sea, stay there. Sally isn't the first woman to marry a sailor."

Bob nodded. "That's what I said to her but she's so damned set on my staying put. Her family, too. Sometimes I think it's her family more than her. She seems happy enough with the baby. I don't think she'd miss *me* all that much."

"You'll have to make up your own mind," said Jim, who preferred Bob to be at sea. They would be separated for long periods, but then he would be separated from Sally too. "How about dinner?"

They went to an Italian restaurant and drank a flask of Chianti between them. Soon the circle would close.

"Where do you want to go?" asked Jim when they had finished.

"I don't care. Anyplace I can get drunk."

"There's a bar I know."

They walked through the warm night air to a bar where men hunted men. Jim was curious to see how Bob would react. They took a table and ordered whiskey. There were enough women present to disguise to the casual observer the nature of the place.

Bob looked about him. "Not too many women here," he said at last.

"No, not so many. Do you want one?"

Bob laughed. "Hey, I'm a married man. Remember?"

"That's why I brought you here. No temptation."

They drank and talked. Their old intimacy was resumed, which meant that Bob did most of the talking, while Jim listened and waited. Bob talked of life at sea, and Jim watched the comedy at the bar. An Air Force pilot would squeeze in beside a sailor. They would talk, legs pressed together. Then they would leave, faces flushed, eyes bright.

Youth drawn to youth, unlike the sad old men, eager but unattractive, who tried first one boy, then another; inured to rebuff, they searched always for that exceptional type which liked old men, or money.

"That's sort of a queer-looking crowd," said Bob suddenly, motioning to the bar.

"Just New York." Jim was a little frightened. Suppose Bob panicked? Had he overplayed his hand?

"I guess that *is* New York. Full of queers. They seem to be everywhere now. Even onboard ship. Once I had a skipper who was, but he never bothered me. He liked niggers. I guess it takes all kinds. Want another drink?" Bob ordered another round.

Jim was relieved at Bob's display of tolerance.

"You know any women?" asked Bob finally. "I mean just to talk to. Sally'd kill me if I ever did anything else. That's why, believe it or not, I've only shacked up with one other woman since I married, which is a pretty good record. No, I just mean girls for company."

"Yes. But they'd be all tied up this late."

"I guess it's pretty short notice. Of course I know a few numbers. Maybe I ought to call them."

Jim thought it wise to make no protest.

"Let's go over to my hotel." Bob stood up. "I'll call from there." They paid for their drinks and left the bar. Envious eyes watched them depart.

They crossed Times Square. Hot windless night. Lights flashing. People everywhere. The mood jubilant, postwar. Bob's hotel was on a side street. They went straight to his room. As Jim stepped inside, he was suddenly overwhelmed by Bob's physical reality. Clothes were strewn about the floor, a damp towel hung from the bathroom door, the bed was a tangle of sheets, and over the harsh odor of disinfec-

tant and dust, Jim was aware of Bob's own smell, to him
erotic.

"Kind of a mess," said Bob mechanically. "I'm not very
neat. Sally always gets mad at the way I throw things
around." He went to the telephone and placed several calls.
No one was home. Finally, he put the receiver down and
grinned. "I guess I was meant to be good tonight. So let's
get drunk. Might as well be drunk as the way we are." He
took a bottle from his suitcase and poured two drinks.
"Here's how." He drank his shot at a gulp. Jim merely
tasted the whiskey. He had to keep clearheaded.

As they drank beneath the harsh unshaded light of a
single electric bulb, the room became stifling with summer
heat. They took off their shirts. Bob's body was still muscular and strong, the skin smooth and white, not freckled,
unlike most redheads.

The duet began pianissimo.

"You remember the old slave cabin?" asked Jim.

"Down by the river? Sure."

"We had a lot of fun there."

"I'll say. There was a pond, too, wasn't there? Where we
swam?"

Jim nodded. "Remember the last time we were there?"

"No, I don't think I do."

Could he have forgotten? Impossible. "Sure you remember. The weekend before you went North. Right after you
graduated."

Bob nodded. "Yeah, I kind of remember." He frowned.
"We . . . we fooled around quite a bit, didn't we?"

Yes, he remembered. Now it would happen. "Yes. Kind
of fun, wasn't it?"

Bob chuckled.

"I guess we were just a couple of little queers at heart."

"Did you ever . . . well, do *that* again, with anybody else?"

"Any other guy? Hell, no. Did you?"

"No."

"Let's have another drink."

Soon they were both drunk and Bob said that he was sleepy. Jim said that he was, too, and that he had better go home, but Bob insisted that he spend the night with him. They threw their clothes on the floor. Wearing only shorts, they tumbled onto the unmade bed. Bob lay sprawled on his back, arm across his face, apparently unconscious. Jim stared at him: was he really asleep? Boldly, Jim put his hand on Bob's chest. The skin was as smooth as he remembered. Lightly he touched the stray coppery hairs which grew below the deep-set navel. Then, carefully, like a surgeon performing a delicate operation, he unbuttoned Bob's shorts. Bob stirred, but did not wake, as Jim opened wide the shorts to reveal thick blond pubic hair from which sprouted the pale quarry. Slowly his hand closed around Bob's sex. He held him for what seemed a long time. Held him, until he looked up to find that the other was awake and watching him. Jim's heart stopped for a full beat.

"What the fuck are you doing?" The voice was hard. Jim could not speak. Obviously the world was ending. His hand remained frozen where it was. Bob pushed him. But he could not move.

"Let go of me, you queer."

Plainly a nightmare, Jim decided. None of this could be happening. But when Bob struck him hard in the face, the pain recalled him. Jim drew back. Bob leapt to his feet and stood, swaying drunkenly, fumbling with buttons. "Now will you get the hell out of here?"

Jim touched his face where he had been struck. His head still rang from the blow. Was he bleeding?

"Get out, you hear me?" Bob moved toward him, menacingly, fist ready. Suddenly, overwhelmed equally by rage and desire, Jim threw himself at Bob. They grappled. They fell across the bed. Bob was strong but Jim was stronger. Grunting and grasping, they twisted and turned, struck out with arms, legs, but Bob was no match for Jim and, at the end, he lay facedown on the bed, arm bent behind him, sweating and groaning. Jim looked down at the helpless body, wanting to do murder. Deliberately he twisted the arm he held. Bob cried out. Jim was excited at the other's pain. What to do? Jim frowned. Drink made concentration difficult. He looked at the heaving body beneath him, the broad back, ripped shorts, long muscled legs. One final humiliation: with his free hand, Jim pulled down the shorts, revealing white, hard, hairless buttocks. "Jesus," Bob whispered. "Don't. Don't."

Finished, Jim lay on the still body, breathing hard, drained of emotion, conscious that the thing was done, the circle completed, and finished.

At last Jim sat up. Bob did not stir. He remained facedown, clutching the pillow to his face while Jim dressed. Then Jim crossed to the bed and looked down at the body he had loved with such single-mindedness for so many years. Was this all? He put his hand on Bob's sweaty shoulder. Bob shied away from him: fear? disgust? It made no difference now. Jim touched the pillow. It was wet. Tears? Good. Without a word, Jim went to the door and opened it. He looked back once more at Bob, then he turned out the light and shut the door behind him. He left the hotel, not caring where he went. For a long time he walked aimlessly, until at last he came to one of the many bars where men looked for men. He entered, prepared to drink until the dream was completely over.

CHAPTER
11

IT WAS LATE, VERY late. He had begun to forget again. Only by great effort had he been able to remember what had happened to him. Now he felt no sorrow. Nothing. Bob was finished and that was the end of that.

He called to the bartender. The man came over. "Another one?"

Jim nodded. His head felt strangely heavy. If he nodded too hard it might fall off. "Another one."

Then a little man with a dark mustache and quick-moving eyes came up. "May I sit down? Could I buy you a drink?"

"If you want to."

"It's certainly been warm weather, hasn't it? I'm from Detroit myself. Where are you from?"

"I forgot."

"Oh, I'm sorry if I'm intruding. I didn't mean to pry."

"All right." Jim was glad to have someone sitting opposite him. Someone who liked to talk. The sound of words was peaceful if one didn't attend to their meaning.

"Isn't this a big town, though? I've been here maybe two weeks and still don't feel I've seen a thing. It's much bigger than Detroit and there seems to be everything here. I've never seen so much of *everything*. Do you work here, if I'm not being too personal?"

"Yes." Jim wondered how long it would take the waiter to bring him his drink. He could make no contact with reality or even unreality until he had another drink. Suddenly there was a glass in front of him. Jim took a swallow: cold, hot, cold, hot. That's the way it should be. He looked at the small man. He had a feeling that a question had been asked, for the little man sat looking at him. He wondered if he had heard the question and forgotten it or whether he had never heard it at all. "You say something?"

"I only asked if you lived here in town."

"Yes." Now the next question. The catechism never changed.

"Do you live with your family?"

"No."

"Then you're not married?"

"No." Jim decided that he would play for a while. Lead the man on and then pretend anger and frighten him. It would be amusing.

"Well, neither am I. You know, I've always said it's a lot cheaper to buy milk than keep a cow." He paused as though expecting either laughter or agreement. He got neither. "I'll bet they've got some good-looking girls around here." The little man winked at Jim. "I'll bet you have a girl here."

"I don't have a girl." Jim offered hope.

"Now that's strange, a young fellow like you. Were you in the Army?"

"Yes," said Jim, and he took another swallow. Everything was pleasant and warm inside his stomach. But his knees felt odd, disconnected. Then the little man put his foot next to his. Deliberately Jim picked up his own foot and, after a long thoughtful minute, brought it down hard on the little man's foot.

"Ouch!"

"Sorry." Jim was happy that he had caused pain.

"You've certainly had a lot to drink."

"How can you tell?"

"I mean . . . well, you seem to have had a lot to drink." The little man paused uneasily. "By the way," he said, "I've got a bottle of real Scotch up in my room at the hotel. If you'd care to . . ."

"I like it here."

"I just thought maybe you might like to come up for a little while, that's all. We could have a friendly chat and it's certainly much nicer there than it is here."

Jim glared at him. "You think I'm trade maybe? You think maybe I'll go home with a little fag like you, maybe? Or do you want to get me drunk in case I'm straight, and screw me?"

His brief acquaintance stood up. "Now, really, I think you've gone far enough. If you weren't drunk you wouldn't say such things to me. Such a thought never entered my mind. If you'll excuse me . . ." The man went away and Jim started to laugh. He laughed loudly for several moments and then he stopped, wanting to cry or sob or shout. But the bartender put an end to that. He came over and told him that the bar was closing and it was time to go.

Unsteadily, Jim walked out into the damp air of early

morning. It was very dark. There were no stars; no moon; only streetlamps shining in the blackness.

Then he was sober.

The edges of the buildings became sharp and clear. He knew exactly where he was and who he was and there was nothing left to do but continue, as though nothing had happened. But even as he made this vow, he recalled firelight and heard again the river's roar. No vision ended except in something vivid and new, and there was nothing new for him. The lover and brother was gone, replaced by a memory of bruised flesh, tangled sheets, violence. Panicky, he contemplated flight. He would return to sea. Change his name, memories, life. He turned west toward the waterfront. Yes, he would ship out again and travel in strange countries and meet new people. Begin again.

Then suddenly he was on the docks, with silent ships all about him. The air was cool. The morning near. At his feet the waters rose and fell slowly, gently, like the breathing of some vast monster. Once more he stood beside a river, aware at last that the purpose of rivers is to flow into the sea. Nothing that ever was changes. Yet nothing that is can ever be the same as what went before. Fascinated, he watched the water shifting dark and cold against the stony island. Soon he would move on.

ALSO BY GORE VIDAL

THE NARRATIVES OF EMPIRE SERIES

Gore Vidal's Narratives of Empire series spans the history of the United States from the Revolution to the post–World War II years. With their broad canvas and large cast of fictional and historical characters, the novels in this series present the American experience as interpreted by one of its most knowing and ironic observers.

BURR

Burr is a portrait of perhaps the most complex and misunderstood of the Founding Fathers. In 1804, while serving as vice president, Aaron Burr fought a duel with his political nemesis, Alexander Hamilton, and killed him. In 1807, he was arrested, tried, and acquitted of treason. In 1833, Burr is newly married, an aging statesman considered a monster by many. But he is determined to tell his own story. With Charles Shuyler, a young journalist whom Burr has chosen as an assistant, he explores both his own past and the continuing political intrigues of the still young United States.

Historical Fiction/Literature/0-375-70873-1

LINCOLN

To most Americans, Abraham Lincoln is seen as the Great Emancipator, beloved by all. In *Lincoln* we meet Lincoln the man. Far from steadfast in his abhorrence of slavery, Lincoln agonizes over the best course of action and comes to his great decision only when all else seems to fail. As the Civil War ravages his nation, Lincoln must face the loss of his dearest son, and the harangues of a wife seen as a traitor for her Southern connections. Brilliantly conceived and executed, *Lincoln* allows the man to breathe again.

Historical Fiction/Literature/0-375-70876-6

1876

The centennial of the United States was celebrated with great fanfare—fireworks, exhibitions, and perhaps the most underhanded political machination in the country's history: the theft of the presidency from Samuel Tilden in favor of Rutherford B. Hayes. This was the Gilded Age, when robber barons held the nation's purse strings. *1876* gives us the era through the eyes of Charlie Schuyler, who has returned from exile to regain a lost fortune, only to find that the effects of corruption reach deep, even into his own family.

Historical Fiction/Literature/0-375-70872-3

this breathtaking epic, Vidal recreates America's Gilded Age—a period of promise and possibility, of empire-building and fierce political rivalries. As the fortunes of a sister and brother intertwine with the fates of their generation, their country, and the greatest names of the day—including Theodore Roosevelt, William and Henry James, the Astors, the Vanderbilts, and the Whitneys—Vidal sweeps us from the nineteenth century into the twentieth, from the salvaged republic of Lincoln to a nation boldly reaching for the world.

Historical Fiction/Literature/0-375-70874-X

HOLLYWOOD

The time is 1917. In Washington, President Wilson is about to lead the United States into the Great War. In California, a new industry is born that will transform America: moving pictures. Here is history brimming with intrigue and scandal, peopled by the greats of the silver screen and American politics, from Charlie Chaplin and Douglas Fairbanks to Franklin D. Roosevelt and the author's own grandfather, the blind Senator Gore. With *Hollywood*, Vidal once again proves himself a superb storyteller and chronicler of history.

Historical Fiction/Literature/0-375-70875-8

THE GOLDEN AGE

The Golden Age is Vidal's stunning tapestry of American political and cultural life from 1939 to 1954, when the epochal events of World War II and the Cold War transformed America, for good or ill, from a republic into an empire. Vidal offers up U.S. history as only he can, with unrivaled wit, and high drama, allied to a classical view of human fate. It is a supreme entertainment that will change readers' understanding of American history and power.

Historical Fiction/Literature/0-375-72481-8

WASHINGTON, D.C.

Washington, D.C., the final installment in Vidal's acclaimed series of historical novels about the American past, offers an illuminating portrait of our republic from the time of the New Deal to the McCarthy era. A stunning tale of diseased ambition, it traces the fortunes of James Burden Day, a powerful senator with his eye on the presidency; Clay Overbury, a young congressional aide with his own political aspirations; and Blaise Sanford, a ruthless newspaper tycoon who understands the importance of money and image in modern politics.

Historical Fiction/Literature/0-375-70877-4